RHYTHM OF THREE

KELLY JAMIESON

Praise for Kelly Jamieson

"Kelly Jamieson delivers a blazing passionate read that tugs at the heartstrings!" **Carly Phillips, *New York Times* Best-selling Author**

"seductive and bewitching from the very start ... Softly romantic and wickedly provocative" ***RT Book Reviews* on Rule of Three**

"Kelly Jamieson now has a permanent place on my keeper shelf and I can't wait to see what she writes next." **Joyfully Reviewed**

"Ms. Jamieson once again gives the reader a richly detailed story that is brimming over with sexual tension, intoxicating desires and intriguing carnal needs that is edgy and psychologically intense..." **The Romance Studio**

"...I love Kelly Jamieson's books and the way that she depicts her characters..." **Sizzling Hot Book Reviews**

This is for everyone who wanted more of Kassidy, Chris and Dag's story
—thank you for loving them as much as I do!

Chapter One

"Do I have to go to work?"

Kassidy burrowed under the covers, her front pressed up against a hard male back, her arm around his middle. Behind her, Chris's body warmed her, his fingers stroking hair off her cheek.

"Yeah," Chris whispered. The voice of Katy Perry emanated from the clock radio beside the bed. Damn that alarm clock. "Sorry, sweetheart."

"I think we should take a sick day." The hard male body beneath her arm began to shake and then Dag shifted, rolling to face her. He propped one hand up on an elbow and smiled down at her.

"You feel sick?"

Kassidy met the gleam of laughter in his dark eyes. "No. I just want to stay here in bed with you guys all day."

Two men. In her bed. And she didn't want to leave.

After all the emotion and drama of the last few days, it was hard to believe that things were more or less settled now. Well, as settled as they could be, when three people were embarking on a *ménage à trois* relationship that still boggled the mind. All she knew was she didn't want it any other way.

"I've got a big meeting at nine," Chris said, now stroking a hand over her shoulder. She felt his lips, warm on her shoulder blade. "Can't call in sick."

"I've got a flight to make," Dag said.

Kassidy froze, eyes flying open wide despite her fatigue. "What?"

"Kidding." He touched her nose. "I'll cancel the flight."

She closed her eyes briefly. He'd planned to leave Chicago, with a flight booked to San Francisco that he very nearly had ended up taking.

"Asshole," Chris said behind her.

Dag grinned. "I was joking, but at some point I'll have to go back to San Francisco. I still have my apartment and all my stuff there. Gonna have to deal with that."

"Oh." Kassidy let out a soft exhalation. "Of course. That's going to be a big job."

"Uh…yeah. Got a lot of shit. Furniture. Clothes. Computer stuff."

Kassidy squinted at Dag in the dim bedroom, even as Chris continued to caress her shoulder and arm. "What are you going to do with it all?"

Dag pursed his lips. "Not sure." He grimaced. "Haven't had much of a chance to think about it."

Of course he hadn't. Only last night they'd all agreed he was going to move in with her and Chris. Their new condo was nice, and even had three bedrooms, but there certainly wasn't room for a whole bunch more furniture. But it didn't seem right that Dag had to give up all his stuff. Unless maybe he lived a sparse bachelor lifestyle and his furniture consisted of a leather recliner chair and big screen TV.

"Maybe we could all go back with you and help," Kassidy suggested, partly curious about his life in San Francisco.

His eyes warmed. "Yeah. Maybe."

She shifted in the bed so she was on her back between her two guys. "D'you guys think we should move to a new place?"

They both stared at her.

"Uh, why, hon?" Chris asked. "We just bought this place."

She hitched one bare shoulder, glancing at Dag, then back to him. They'd talked about this briefly last night. "I know," she said softly. "We did just buy it, and I love it. But this is *our* place. As in, you and me," she said to Chris. "Maybe it would be nice to have a place that really belongs to all three of us."

"I'll pay the mortgage payment," Dag said immediately.

"Fuck off, you will not," Chris snapped.

"You don't have to do that," she said to Dag, a gentler way of reiterating Chris's comment.

"I can afford it," Dag said. "Why not?"

"You're not supporting us," Chris clipped. "That's not what this is about."

"I fucking know that," Dag said, eyes narrowing.

"Okay, this isn't the time to discuss this," she said, lifting her hands to touch both their chests. "Clearly, we still have a lot of things to figure out. We can talk more tonight over dinner."

She felt a little of the tension ease out of both their bodies and then she got a kiss on each cheek. She closed her eyes, pleasure filtering through her as they leaned in and kissed her —three of them together in the big bed, the soft sheets wrapped around them, their body heat warming her, their individual scents combining in a heady, sexy fragrance. She really did just want to stay there all day, with them. She sighed.

"We've got forever, babe," Dag whispered. "Right?"

She smiled at him, the impatient, reckless one, counseling her about patience. "Right."

"I'm grabbing the shower," Chris said. His hand on her belly slid up between her breasts to her jaw, turned her face toward him and his mouth captured hers in a hard, fast kiss. Then he climbed out of bed and disappeared into the bathroom off their master bedroom. She couldn't help watching his big, naked body, admiring the flex of muscle in his ass and thighs. When she turned her gaze back to Dag, he was watching Chris too.

They smiled at each other. "He's hot," she whispered.

"Yeah." Dag's fingertips cruised over her cheek and jaw. "He is. And so are you."

Heat washed down through her. "I have meetings today too," she whispered as Dag wrapped his arms around her and rolled to his back with her on top of him. "How the hell am I going to concentrate on work?"

"Hmmm." Dag nuzzled the side of her neck. Her skin tingled everywhere. "You can do it."

"Guess I have to." She tried to pull away, but his arms tightened. "'Kay, let me go. I need coffee."

He landed one big hand on her butt in a little spank that weirdly felt good. She wriggled on him, felt his cock stir and grinned.

"Get out of here," he growled. "Before I make you late for work."

Still smiling, she slid off the bed and found her silky robe where she'd dropped it over the arm of the chair yesterday. Barefoot, she meandered out of the bedroom, the hardwood floors of their condo cool and smooth beneath her feet. In the open concept kitchen/dining/living room, sun flooded in the front windows, dappled by the maple trees that lined their street. Beyond the green leaves, the sky was clear blue. A gorgeous June day.

Holy crap. She paused at the kitchen counter and her head

whipped around to look at the calendar on the wall. With everything that had gone on the last few days, she'd completely forgotten Chris's birthday was this Thursday.

His thirtieth birthday. A milestone.

She needed to do something about that.

She added water to the TASSIMO, popped in a T DISC and started the appliance to brew her cup of coffee. Dag would drink a Coke—if they had any. Things had been a little unsettled the last few days.

Saturday night they'd had a party to celebrate her parents' thirtieth wedding anniversary, although it had been a tiny party since her mom was still recovering from her car accident. At the party, Kassidy had had that run-in with Hailey, her sister, which had been upsetting. Then the next day, Chris had kicked Dag out of their home. Their threesomes had never included the guys having sex—until that night, when Dag had initiated it, and Chris hadn't been ready to face his feelings for Dag. That had been even more upsetting. After that, everything was kind of foggy. She had no idea if they had food in the cabinets or Coke in the fridge.

She drifted across the small kitchen and opened the fridge door. Oh thank heaven, a couple of cans of Coke sat on the top shelf, along with the beer Chris and Dag both liked. She surveyed the other contents of the fridge, trying to plan a meal for that night. God, she hadn't even cooked dinner Sunday or Monday night. She'd been too distraught to eat lunch on Monday and might have eaten a few crackers Monday night, but again she'd been so upset, she hadn't been interested in food at all.

But she'd done some shopping Saturday before the party and she found some chicken breasts, some tomatoes and peppers. She had pasta in the cupboard and a loaf of crusty bread they'd never even cut into... They were good for tonight.

Chris emerged from the bedroom, damp hair combed back off his face, dressed in his suit pants and shirt. He was fastening the buttons at his wrists, his tie hanging loose around his neck.

"Want coffee?" she asked him, admiring his broad shoulders beneath the crisp blue fabric of his shirt.

"Mmm, yeah. Americano."

She popped another T DISC into the TASSIMO and slipped another mug under it, then picked up hers and sipped it. "Dag in the shower? Or can I use the bathroom now?"

"He was still in bed."

Their eyes met.

She drifted toward him and laid her hand on the side of his neck. "Okay, honey?" she murmured.

He closed his eyes briefly. This was pretty fucking enormous for him. "Okay."

"I love you."

"Love you too. So much, Kass."

His hands reached for her hips and pulled her to him. Mindful of the mug of coffee she held, she let him press her body against his and kiss her again—this time, deeper, longer, a kiss full of so much emotion.

"I know it's crazy," she whispered to him. "But it's what we all want. What we all need. Right?"

He nodded, forehead against hers. "Yeah. I'm just... I could freak out again if I let myself."

"Don't let yourself."

They both smiled. "I'll work on that," he said, voice gruff.

"Remember. We're both here for you. Dag and I."

"I know. Christ." He closed his eyes.

She looked up at the sound of quiet footsteps and saw Dag standing in the door opening of the kitchen, one shoulder leaning against the frame. Bare-chested, he wore only a pair of boxers that sat low on his lean hips. He was also worthy of some serious studying with his smooth, dark skin and sleek muscles. She met his eyes. Was this okay? She and Chris having a moment alone in the kitchen?

They'd talked a little about how none of them could be jealous. But talk was easy…

Dag's eyes crinkled at the corners as they met hers, his gaze warm. Nope. No jealousy. He straightened and moved toward them. He set a hand on Chris's upper back, rubbing up and down a little, his other hand coming to Kassidy's shoulder, almost embracing both of them. "Got any Coke?" he asked.

She grinned at him. "Yeah."

He kissed her forehead and then headed to the fridge.

She met Chris's eyes again and his mouth lifted into a grin too. "Fucking weird," he muttered.

"Who's weird?" Dag demanded. He popped open the can of soda with a snap and a hiss. "I'm not weird."

"We're all fuckin' weird," Chris said. "That coffee done?"

"Yeah." She reached for it and handed it to him. "We might need to make a bathroom schedule," she said. "I mean, we do have two bathrooms, but—"

"Shower's not big enough for three," Dag commented with a frown. "Unfortunately."

She laughed. "Come on. We can't shower together every day."

"No?" Dag's eyes gleamed as he drank his Coke

"No," she said firmly. "Please. Leave me a little feminine mystery. I'm not shaving in front of you guys, or…or other stuff I do. I need some me time. And probably not only in the shower," she added.

Dag's eyes warmed. "Sure, babe. Whatever you need."

"Right now I need to get ready for work. Unlike you guys, it takes me a long time."

"Go on," Dag said. "I'm not on a schedule like you two are. At least not yet. And hopefully never."

Kassidy laughed as she swept past him and Chris. Dag liked to be his own boss, never one to work a nine-to-five job, sitting in an office. When he'd first come to visit, she'd thought he mocked Chris for his paid employment—even though Chris was ambitious and goal-oriented, and becoming Vice President of Product Development before he was thirty years old was quite an accomplishment. Turned out Dag respected Chris and his hard work and ambition, even though it looked different than his own.

She took her coffee with her to the bedroom and did her morning routine, still in a bit of a daze about all that had happened. She couldn't seem to wipe the smile off her face as she put on makeup and blow-dried her hair. Finally dressed in a spring suit of pale pink with a silky, sleeveless pink blouse beneath the jacket, she rejoined Chris where he sat reading the newspaper, a plate beside him with crumbs indicating he'd eaten some toast. Dag was stretched out on the couch, still in his boxers, drinking a Coke and watching a morning news show.

"I'm ready," she announced.

She and Chris both worked for the same company so they drove to and from work together every day. Chris had a VP parking spot in the underground garage of the office tower in downtown Chicago. Kassidy was a lowly Training and Development Coordinator and did not rate a parking spot. But she loved her job.

She bent over the back of the couch to kiss Dag. "We'll see you later."

He smiled up at her, glanced at Chris shrugging into his suit jacket. "Okay, kids."

Chris paused, watching her kiss Dag goodbye. "I'm not kissing him goodbye," he muttered.

Her eyes went wide but Dag grinned. "I know you love me," he said. "Asshole."

She sucked in a deep breath. Okay, yeah, lots to get used to. They were figuring this out as they went, and today was Day One.

The drive to work was like any other day, she and Chris together in the car, listening to music and news. They rode up the elevator together, and she got off on the eighth floor where Human Resources and Training and Development had their offices, while he continued up to the executive offices on twelve. They didn't kiss goodbye in the elevator because it was full of coworkers. Everyone at RBM Technologies knew they were a couple, of course; it wasn't secret. But PDAs in the elevator weren't exactly professional and although in private Chris was extremely physical and couldn't keep his hands off her, in public, especially at work, he was more circumspect.

Unlike Dag.

Heat washed down beneath her silky blouse as she walked to her office, remembering that night at Kiss, the night everything had started, the night Dag had danced with her and put his hands all over her and slid her skirt up, giving Chris a show...

She shook her head to clear it and make herself focus on business as she walked along the carpeted hall.

What would all those coworkers in the elevator think if they knew not only was she sleeping with the VP of Product Development, but also with his...friend? Her insides tightened. They'd talked a little about this last night—what they were going to tell the world. And basically they'd decided they weren't going to tell the world anything at this point. Which was great, because she didn't even have words to explain it.

She passed her boss Paul's office and called out a good morning.

"Morning, Kassidy. Hey…you feeling better today?"

She'd had a small meltdown the day before, so upset about Dag leaving, and her cheeks warmed. Crying in the office was so unprofessional and Paul had been uncomfortable, albeit concerned. She faced Paul with a small grimace. "Yes," she said. "I am. Sorry about the meltdown. Things have been really stressful lately…with my mom and all." She couldn't exactly tell him the real reason for her tears.

He nodded sympathetically. "I understand. She's doing okay?"

"Yes, she's getting better and better every day. She has a doctor appointment this week I may need to take her to, but hopefully my dad can do it." Her mom had been injured in a bad car accident a few weeks earlier and was recovering from a fractured pelvis.

"Sure, sure. Just let me know."

"Thanks." With a smile she turned away and entered her own small office. Okay. Work. She'd looked at those training proposals yesterday but none of it had stuck in her head, she'd been so sick with worry and distracted about what was happening with Dag and Chris. She grinned. She was still distracted—but for an entirely different reason.

Chapter Two

DAG WATCHED CHRIS AND KASSIDY WALK OUT OF THE CONDO, then let his head drop back to the cushion.

Yeah, this was fucking weird.

When he'd decided to come back to Chicago about six weeks ago, he'd never in his wildest fantasies imagined this was how things would turn out. Yeah, he'd had some cracked, crazy hope that he'd come back and find Chris single and...well, he hadn't even really fully formulated that hope because it had been so fucking hope*less*. Chris was as straight as the Sears Tower—or whatever they called it now—his best buddy, yeah, but in no way interested in anything other than friendship. When Dag had met Kassidy, he'd seen how in love with her Chris was and Dag's heart had turned stone-cold. He'd seen right away that Chris and Kassidy had something real and solid and forever.

Now...was he actually a part of that?

He closed his eyes as his chest squeezed the air out of his lungs. That wasn't panic...was it?

He'd never been in a real relationship. He'd fucked around

most of his life, mostly because he couldn't have the one guy he cared about—Chris. What if he couldn't do this? What if he fucked it up? He'd been so sure he'd already done that on Sunday when Chris told him to get out, when Kassidy had come to see him in the hotel. He'd worried that not only had he fucked up things once and for all between him and Chris, maybe he'd screwed over Kassidy too. Remembering the raw agony of that made him wince.

But relationships were scary and in a way this one was even scarier because he was opening himself up to two people, therefore increasing the risk of getting his heart stomped on.

Not going there. This was one of those "too good to be true" things, but he wasn't going to be his usual self and screw things up because he didn't feel he deserved to be happy. This time he was going to grab this with both hands and hang on and try his damndest to be the kind of man Chris and Kassidy both deserved.

He rolled off the couch, took his empty can to the sink and rinsed it, then tossed it in the recycling box. He looked around the kitchen. This was going to be his place now. Wow.

He thought about Kassidy's comment earlier about finding another place, one they all chose together. Fuck, she was sweet. Thoughtful.

It was true that he was entering into their already established relationship. He'd noted that last night. But Kassidy had assured him that she and Chris were no longer a couple...they were a triad.

Easy to say...and he believed her, believed that she meant that, but, still, this was all new. Okay, he and Kassidy had been getting to know each other, their relationship building and growing, from a little hostility to friendship and now love. But between Chris and him, this was something entirely fucking new. Fucking fantastic, but new.

So maybe they *should* buy another place. What he'd said had been true—he could afford it. Something that was theirs, something bigger and better...a funky loft condo, maybe.

Or maybe not. Neither of them was into status and ostentation. In fact, Kassidy had been annoyed when he'd ordered a pricey bottle of wine, thinking he was showing off. She didn't give a shit about his money and neither did Chris, and that was just one more thing Dag loved about both of them. He'd met his share of users who liked the fact that he was loaded. And since he never gave a shit about anyone, he was fine with people who liked to hang out with him for that reason because when things ended he didn't have to feel bad.

But, fuck, he had money and he liked to spend it. And he'd like to spend it on the people he cared about.

With Chris and Kassidy both gone to work for the day, he had the place to himself. He wandered from the kitchen to their bedroom, looking around. This wasn't the first time he'd been there alone. He'd been practically living there for weeks. He'd checked out of his hotel and brought his stuff there once before. He blew out a long exhalation as he headed for the shower.

While Dag shaved and showered and shampooed, he planned his day. He was right in the middle of a new start-up, which he'd pretty much resigned himself to continuing back in San Francisco. Now that he was staying in Chicago, and it seemed like it was going to be long term, he could resume his work here. Maybe get some office space. Nail down the financing. Get the prototype up and running and test it out, and start the marketing.

Excitement raced through his veins. He loved the adrenaline rush of starting something new, creating something unique and different, and getting it out in the world. He even loved the element of risk that went along with it. Which was not unlike embarking on an unconventional three-way relationship.

Dag smiled ruefully as he dressed in the clothes he'd worn over here yesterday. He'd changed before leaving the hotel, luckily, because he'd been so goddamn wrecked about everything that had happened he'd been sitting there drinking and unshaven and unshowered when Chris had shown up. He glanced at the time on his cell phone. He could check out before noon and not have to pay for another night.

Then he laughed out loud at his thrift when moments ago he'd been contemplating buying a million-dollar loft condo or something. Christ.

He shoved his cell phone in his pocket, but when he went to leave, he realized he no longer had his key. He'd left it there Sunday when Chris had kicked his ass out.

He looked around, but didn't see the key. "Agh." He pulled out his phone and sent Kassidy a text message. But she was working and might not get back to him right away. Now he was antsy and anxious to get going, to start doing things, and waiting around in the condo did not fit in with his plans.

Luckily, she texted back pretty quickly. *Key's hanging inside the cabinet beside fridge.*

He thumbed back a quick *Thanks* as he walked toward the cupboard.

Seconds later another message from Kassidy arrived. *Thurs is Chris's birthday. We should do something. Ideas?*

He paused. Huh. Right. Chris's birthday. Fuck. He had no ideas.

He opened the cupboard door, recognized the key he'd been using and snagged it. He contemplated Kassidy's question as he called a cab. He had no car there, because when he and Chris had left his hotel yesterday, he'd been drinking pretty heavily so Chris had driven.

That was something else he'd have to take care of—he'd been renting a car the whole time he'd been here. He needed to buy something.

In the back of the cab, he texted Kassidy back that he had no ideas but was open to whatever. He held the phone and looked out the window at passing traffic as he waited for her response. Instead of texting, she called him.

He smiled as he answered the call.

"Hey."

"Hi. I thought I'd call since this is getting involved. I don't want to talk about it later when Chris is around."

"Christ. You're not planning a surprise party, are you?"

She gave a soft laugh. "No. He'd hate that. I guess we could just ask him what he wants to do. I was thinking of calling some of our friends though, maybe get everyone together. We could have a party Friday night. You haven't seen the gang all that much since you've been back."

"No. True." They'd been too busy screwing each other's brains out in the many combinations and permutations you could have with three people.

"It's his thirtieth birthday," she said. "I feel we should do something more than just go out for dinner. Although that would be nice too."

"Is a party going to be a lot of work for you? You just did something for your parents."

"I'm not thinking anything fancy. I'll buy some beer and chips and call it good."

Now he laughed. "Right." As if. The anniversary party for her parents had been just them, and she'd gone all out, making snacks and drinks and seafood to grill on the barbecue.

"Seriously," she said.

"You call people and invite them. Let me take care of the rest."

Silence. He could almost sense her frown. "You're going to plan a party?"

"No, I'm going to hire someone to do it."

"Dag!"

"What?" He leaned back, grinning.

"You can't do that!"

"Why not? That's what party planners are for."

"It's Tuesday. We're doing this Friday."

Amusement warmed him inside. "Okay, I'll just hire a caterer," he said. "And a bartender."

After a beat of silence, she said, "Bartender?"

"Sure."

"That would actually be kind of cool. Um…would that cost a lot?"

"I have no idea. Probably not." He made a face though she couldn't see him. "Hey, maybe your sister would like the job."

Waves of silence assaulted his ear now. He grimaced. Kassidy's sister, Hailey, worked at a popular nightclub as a bartender. Well, that was *one* of her jobs. Jesus. But the two sisters' relationship had been strained lately. It had never been great, but when Hailey'd walked in on Kassidy, Chris and Dag in bed one morning, Kassidy had been horrified and terrified that Hailey would tell her parents.

"I guess I'd have to invite her anyway," Kassidy said now with a sigh. "I have to talk to her."

"Yeah?"

"I went to see her the other night. After…you left. I never told you about my conversation with her."

"No. You didn't."

"I'll tell you about it tonight."

"Okay, babe." His voice went gentle. "Everything okay with her?"

"Yeah. Surprisingly."

"Okay. Party starts at eight o'clock at our place, yeah?"

"If you say so." He heard the smile in her voice.

"Give me a rough head count."

"Um...Jeff and Sarah, Cole and Tyra, Matt, Brandon... uh...Danielle...Hailey. Us. That's..."

"Eleven. Any of those gonna bring a date?"

"Maybe."

"So ten to fifteenish people?"

"I'd invite my parents, but Mom's not up to it, obviously. Oh, I know, also James and Vickie."

"Up to seventeen."

"If they can all come. I'll let you know for sure as soon as I can. Now I have a meeting to get to."

"Perfect timing. I just arrived at the hotel."

"Oh. Okay. I'll talk to you later."

"Later, babe."

He ended the call, paid the taxi driver and strode into the hotel lobby.

Add one more thing to his to-do list for the day. He grinned.

"You should have told me what you needed," Dag said to Kassidy as the three of them moved around the small kitchen that evening, making dinner. "I could've picked stuff up."

Chris watched his buddy—correction, his lover—Christ!— talking to his girlfriend. A hot swelling feeling in his chest threatened again, as it had all day. What the fuck had happened? What had they gotten themselves into?

Not that he had regrets. But, holy fuck, this was game changing. This was life altering. Did he even know who he was anymore? Jesus.

He'd let his best friend fuck him.

He closed his eyes briefly, his hands going still, one holding a loaf of bread, the other a knife. Jesus fucking Christ.

He opened his eyes and shot a sideways glance at Dag, standing at the stove stirring the pot of pasta.

He'd *wanted* his best friend to fuck him. And he wanted him to do it again.

Heat pooled in his groin.

He'd been so fucking distracted all day, drifting off during important meetings, having to ask people to repeat what they'd said. He'd looked at his boss and bizarrely wondered what the CEO of RBM Technologies would think if he knew Chris had taken it up the ass from another man last night. He was trying to make sense of it all, questioning his sexuality, trying to decide if he'd just come out of the closet, or if he'd ever even been in the closet, for fuck's sake.

He hadn't known.

And yet, somewhere in the very dark recesses of his consciousness, he had. He had known all along that he wanted Dag.

He'd just closed that part of his brain off.

"I think I need to see a shrink," he announced.

Kassidy and Dag both turned to level him with wide-eyed looks.

"What?" Kassidy said.

Dag choked. "What the fuck, man?"

He let out a short breath. "I'm kidding. Sort of. I'm just trying to figure out what's wrong with me."

Dag's eyes narrowed and his eyebrows pulled together. *"What's wrong with you?"* he asked very slowly, jaw tight.

"Oh, Chris." Kassidy set down the plates she'd lifted from the cupboard and scooted over to him. She wrapped her arms around his middle and hugged him. "There's nothing wrong with you."

"Fuck that bullshit," Dag said roughly. "She's right. There's nothing wrong with you. Don't even fucking go there, because if there's something wrong with you, then—"

"That's not what I mean!" Christ rubbed his forehead. "I don't mean now. That's not what I'm saying. I mean...why didn't I know? Why didn't I ever let myself admit how I felt? What I wanted...from you?"

"I think you know why," Dag said quietly.

Kassidy tipped her head back and gazed up at him.

Chris circled his arms around her and met her eyes. "There are some things I didn't tell you. Yesterday."

She nodded, holding his gaze steadily. "That's okay. We have all the time in the world."

"Kassidy didn't tell me about her conversation with Hailey either," Dag said, moving toward them. He did that triad hug thing again, a hand on the middle of Chris's back, big and warm and strong, another arm around Kassidy. "We still have a lot to talk about."

"Not good at that," Chris reminded them.

"We know, honey," Kassidy said. "We're here to help you."

"Yeah," Dag affirmed. "But, Jesus, if there was ever a time for communication, this is it, man."

"Let's eat dinner first," Kassidy said. "And talk after. And, Chris...if you seriously want to see someone for help making sense of all this, there's nothing wrong with that. Just don't... don't think there's something wrong with you. Please."

He nodded and gave her a squeeze before releasing her. "Okay."

Shit. He was gonna fuck this up. He resumed slicing the bread, then spread it with the garlic butter Kassidy had whipped up.

"Wrap it in foil," she told him. "We'll warm it up in the oven."

"Pasta's done," Dag said.

"Perfect."

They were soon sitting down at the dining table with steaming plates of pasta primavera and garlic bread.

"Okay," Kassidy said. "Birthday plans."

Chris's head jerked up. "Birthday? My birthday?"

"No, Halle Berry's birthday," she said with an eye-roll.

Chris couldn't help but smile. "Halle Berry's coming to celebrate my birthday with me? *Sweet.*"

"You wish."

Chris relaxed a little. "Damn."

"Big three-oh," Dag said. "Old fucker."

Chris smirked. "I'm less than a month older than you. And I'm in better shape."

"Fuck that."

"Better start taking your vitamins."

Dag snorted. Kassidy laughed. And a little more tension eased out of Chris.

"We're having a party here Friday night," Kassidy said.

"We are?" Chris lifted his eyebrows at her.

"Yes! It's going to be so fun! Dag's hiring a bartender."

Chris blinked at Kassidy, then turned his gaze on Dag. "Uh…okay."

Dag grinned.

"He's already talked to a caterer," Kassidy continued. "So it won't be much work. That was sweet of you," she added, fluttering her eyelashes at Dag.

"You've been busting your ass looking after everyone else," Dag said. "I got this, Kass."

Warmth spread in Chris's chest. Fuck, he liked that Dag cared so much about Kassidy. "Thanks, man," he said quietly. "When did this all come about?"

"Today," Kassidy replied cheerfully, stabbing a piece of

penne with her fork. "I knew your birthday was coming, but things have been so crazy lately—"

"There's an epic understatement," Dag said.

She grinned. "I just realized this morning that it's Thursday. So Dag and I talked about what to do and we decided to have a party. Casual, just our friends. I've invited everyone already. They can all come, except Hailey, she has to work."

"Maybe just as well...?" Chris said.

Kassidy looked down at her plate. "You know, she was pretty helpful the other night when I was so upset. I didn't know who else to go to, to talk about this. I didn't think I could go to Danielle about it." Kassidy's best friend, who had no idea what was going on.

"Danielle coming to the party?" Chris asked.

"Yeah."

He set down his fork. "Guess we're going to have to talk about how that's going to go."

"Add it to the list of discussion topics," Dag said.

"Jesus," Chris muttered. "Should we create an agenda?"

"You're the businessman," Dag said. "Also, you're the oldest. You might need an agenda to remember everything we need to discuss."

Chris couldn't help it. He burst out laughing. "Oh man. I meant, do we have to make this so complicated?"

"Uh...dude," Dag murmured. "This *is* pretty fuckin' complicated."

Chris rubbed the back of his neck where tightness was again starting to climb up his scalp. "Yeah," he said on a sigh. "I know. I just don't want to talk about all this shit."

"What do you want to do?" Dag asked, eyes gleaming.

Heat burst and rushed through Chris's body. What the hell. Might as well be honest. "I wanna fuck around."

Chapter Three

"RIGHT, THEN. WE'LL TALK LATER." DAG PUSHED HIS CHAIR back.

Kassidy's eyes moved back and forth between the two men. Heat had been building all through dinner. She'd been tense about Chris, concerned with some of the things he'd said, worried about him not opening up to them. Of all of them, this was the most momentous for him.

Well, maybe for her too. Wow. Weird that she was all worried about Chris, and here she was in a ménage à trois relationship with two guys.

Yeah, that was significant. But for Chris…definitely more so.

"Guys," she said. "Cool your jets. We need to talk." But even though she said it, her pussy was pulsing and warm, thinking about being back in their bed with two hot, naked men. Two hot, naked men she loved.

Chris looked at her. "Sweetheart. Seriously?"

She rolled her eyes and pushed her own chair back. "Someone has to be sensible."

"Fuck sensible," Dag said. "I was never a big fan of sensible."

"I was," Chris muttered.

Dag grinned and moved toward him to slide a hand around the back of Chris's neck. "You also were a fan of being in control. You hate not being in control...don't you?"

Kassidy watched the two of them, a sweet ache developing low inside her. God, she loved seeing them together. She had from the first night Dag had come to their place, the day they'd gone to a baseball game and come home a little drunk and sunburned, having so much fun. She'd loved watching Chris easily give Dag a one-armed hug, their trash talking, their obvious comfort with each other, which she'd never seen Chris display with another guy.

And now...now he was able to show his real feelings for Dag, the feelings that went way deeper than camaraderie or friendship. She loved that for him.

She also loved it for Dag. Her heart had broken for him when she'd learned that he'd been in love with Chris for so long. He'd never found anyone else, even in all the years he'd lived in LA and San Francisco. He'd hidden it under a layer of cynicism and toughness, but she knew he wanted love just like everyone did.

"Yeah," Chris agreed roughly, eyes focused on Dag's face.

She loved how much Dag got Chris. She'd thought she knew Chris better than anybody, knew his flaws and his strengths, knew how to communicate with him. But since Dag had been back, she'd seen that he too knew all those things—perhaps instinctively, since they'd known each other for so long. Or maybe he'd taken the time to think about Chris and analyze him. Whatever it was, she didn't feel jealous that someone else read him as well as she did—she felt pleased and satisfied. Happy for Chris. And lucky. So damn lucky.

Chris was the one who usually controlled their sex. And Kassidy liked that. Last night, she'd ached for him, how he'd submitted to Dag—and to her, really. He'd been overwhelmed and this had been new to him and he'd been hesitant and maybe a little scared. They'd taken care with him. They'd made it good for him, that she knew. That had been their goal. The newness hadn't only come from the fact that he was having sex with a man for the first time in his life, but also from the fact that he wasn't the one in control.

"You want control?" Dag whispered to him. "Take it." He leaned his forehead against Chris's, hand still wrapped around the back of his neck.

Jesus, sparks practically flew. Kassidy watched the show with rapt attention.

Was Chris ready for that?

"Um…guys?"

They both turned their eyes on her.

"Do you two want to be alone?"

They stared at her. They looked at each other, then back at her.

"Kass," Chris said, his forehead creasing. "Don't you want…?"

"You know I do," she said hastily. "I just thought…this is new for you two…maybe you two should have time together."

"Fuck." Dag closed his eyes. "Kass. You kill me."

She blinked.

"I love that you want to give us that," he said. "I seriously fucking do."

"Me too," Chris said quietly. "But tonight…I want you with us."

She nodded, her heart squeezing. "Okay."

"That is gonna happen," Dag said. "We *are* gonna be alone. Me and Chris. You and me. You and Chris. Right?"

Chris and Kass both breathed out a soft, "Right."

"And we're all gonna be okay with that."

"Yes." Kassidy nodded.

"Yeah," Chris muttered. His gaze shifted back to her. Hot. "Tonight I'm gonna get to know Dag. But you're gonna be there with me."

Her lips parted. "Okay."

Chris grabbed Dag's face and gave him a fast, hard kiss. "Get into the bedroom and get naked."

Kassidy's eyes widened briefly. Whoa.

Dag gave a slow, sexy smile, with that wicked arch of one eyebrow, then turned and left the kitchen.

Chris lifted his chin at Kassidy and she floated across the room and into his arms. "Need you there, sweetheart," he murmured before his mouth found hers.

"Yeah." She knew. Her heart swelled again with love for him. She hugged him tight and kissed him back, then together they turned to follow Dag to the bedroom.

She spared a brief thought for the dishes on the table and in the sink. That they should be practical and clean up before they had hot, dirty sex. Apparently the important discussions they needed to have were also being postponed. But the heat coursing through her veins, the lust pulsing inside her, overrode sensible and responsible.

They walked into the bedroom and her heart halted briefly at seeing Dag lying naked on the bed. He lay on one side, elbow in the mattress, head in his hand, his other hand stroking his enormous erection.

God, he was beautiful, long, lean muscles and tanned skin, dark hair on his thighs and chest, denser at the root of his cock. His freakin' huge cock.

Her heart resumed beating in a rapid rhythm and liquid heat pooled between her legs.

"You get naked too," Chris told her, and she quickly stripped off her T-shirt and shorts, panties and bra. Chris did the same, with slower, deliberate motions.

She admired him too, his bulkier muscles, the golden hair on his arms and legs. He rounded the bed to the far side—*his* side, which made her smile—and set one knee on the mattress. He gestured to the bed on the other side of Dag, and she hurried over to climb on. She sat on the edge of the bed, her butt to her calves, hands on her thighs, waiting for further instruction from Chris.

"Fuck, Dag," Chris breathed, studying him. It seemed he wanted to say more, but didn't, and a moment passed as he let his gaze roam over Dag's body.

"He's gorgeous, isn't he?" Kassidy said softly.

"Yeah. Wanna explore every inch of you," Chris continued. A shiver ran over Kassidy's skin. "Kassidy and I are gonna do that." His gaze flickered to hers and she nodded. "Kiss him."

She obeyed him without question, leaning forward to touch her lips to Dag's. He opened to her immediately, his lips firm and hot, his tongue brushing over her bottom lip. "Mmm."

She drew back and then Chris took his turn, bending to kiss Dag too, and when their mouths met, a surge of red-hot lust burned inside her. She watched with almost unbearable delight as they kissed, their tongues sweeping together, eyes closed, Dag's long, dark eyelashes like fans on his cheekbones.

Heat burned beneath her skin as she watched them, then she couldn't resist touching, stroking one hand up Dag's hard, hairy thigh.

Chris moved his mouth away from Dag's, kissing Dag's jaw, his neck, his shoulder. He brought his hands into action, rubbing them over Dag's chest, his nipples, making Dag suck in a sharp breath. "Like that?" Chris asked.

"Fuck yeah."

"Kassidy's gonna suck you," Chris said.

Kassidy smiled, only too happy to participate. She glanced up at Dag, met his gaze, slicked her tongue over her bottom lip. His eyes had darkened to near black, color riding his cheekbones.

"Yeah," he muttered. "Suck my cock, Kass. Suck it good."

She shifted herself closer. Dag still stroked himself, and he held his shaft upright, offering it to her. She paused for a moment to take in the visual. He had a beautiful cock, definitely well endowed, the head smooth with a defined ridge. As he slowly pumped his hand up and down, she took in the thick veins and the glisten of fluid at the very tip. Her mouth watered, and she closed her eyes and lowered her mouth to taste him.

His essence filled her senses—the taste of him, the scent of him. He released his cock and she took over, closing the fingers of one hand around the base. It pulsed hot against her hand as she swirled her tongue over the tip, lips circling him. Her other hand slipped between his thighs, which he widened to accommodate her.

His skin was hot and damp there, the skin of his inner thighs and his balls thin and tender. She cupped him gently, gave a strong suck, then released him. He needed to be wetter, slipperier, and she spent a moment licking him all over, up and down and around until her hand slid more easily on him. Then she took him in her mouth again, now able to glide her lips lower.

Dag was huge and she already knew there was no hope of taking him very deep, but she also knew he liked whatever she gave him.

She flicked her eyes upward to catch glimpses of Chris kissing Dag's chest, then sucking on his nipples. When he did that, Dag's balls tightened and his cock twitched in her mouth.

She smiled around his thick length, loving the reaction, loving that Chris was doing this.

When Dag reached for Chris, Chris grabbed Dag's arms and shoved them up over his head, licking over Dag's chest, then stroking his tongue over the inside of his upper arms. Dag groaned, head turned on the pillow, eyes closed. Chris skated his hands up Dag's sides, all the way up his arms, ending by giving Dag's mouth a hard kiss, then doing it again, and again.

Kassidy's eyes drifted closed again. Sounds of pleasure filled the room, Kassidy's murmurs of enjoyment, Dag's groans of pleasure and Chris's grunts of happiness. She got lost in all the sensations, the sounds, the clean male taste of Dag, the feel of his cock so heavy and smooth in her mouth, the tightness of his balls. Her head swam with dizziness, her body on fire, a hard, insistent pulse between her legs.

"C'mere, Kass," Chris whispered, reaching for her. Kassidy lifted her head with one last suck, still holding Dag's shaft, mouth wet, breathing heavily, and above Dag, she and Chris kissed. When she drew back, he said, "I can taste him on you."

She gave him a look from beneath her eyelashes. "D'you like that?"

She wanted him to suck Dag too, but apparently that wasn't the plan just then.

"Yeah. I do. Let's play with his ass. Roll over, Dag."

Heat flashed in her belly again as the two of them moved and Dag stretched out on his belly, adjusting himself by shoving a hand underneath himself, which made her nipples tingle and burn. They stroked Dag's back, his ass, the backs of his thighs, admiring him with their hands and their eyes. Kassidy bent to place openmouthed kisses on the small of his back, one on each of the indentations there, then she licked lower and nipped his buttock with her lips. His body jerked.

Chris did the same, exploring with hands and lips and

tongue. He'd never done this before, had probably never realized or acknowledged that he wanted to, and she sensed his rising excitement and delight. He parted Dag's thighs, stroked between his cheeks, brushed his fingers over Dag's balls. With an expression of curiosity and wonder, he leaned in closer, thumbs separating Dag's flesh, studying him, rubbing over Dag's anus. Again, Dag's body twitched and a low sound rumbled from his chest. "Oh yeah," he muttered.

Then Chris groaned and crawled up the bed and fell down beside Dag on his belly. "Want you to fuck me," he whispered to Dag.

"Yeah? You want that again?"

"Yeah."

Dag pushed up to his knees and straddled Chris, who still lay facedown. Without being asked, Kassidy leaned back and reached for the bottle of lube on the table beside the bed. Her eyes met Dag's as she handed it to him, and he gave her a smile of gratitude.

He squeezed the lube onto his fingers then slid them up and down between Chris's cheeks. Chris made another hoarse sound of pleasure.

"Fuck," Dag muttered. Kassidy's gaze dropped to his cock, swollen and ridged with veins. He used his slick hand to stroke himself, then drizzled more of the lubrication onto his shaft. "So glad we agreed no more condoms."

Chris and Kassidy had done away with condoms a long time ago, and Dag had been tested and hadn't been with anyone but Kassidy since then.

"Do it," Chris groaned. "For fuck's sake, I'm coming out of my skin. *Do it.*"

Kassidy's eyes met Dag's again, catching the gleam of amusement there before he moved between Chris's thighs. Kassidy licked her lips, laid her hands on Chris's cheeks to help part them for Dag and watched as gorgeous agony tightened his face. He rubbed the head of his cock over Chris's puckered entrance then sucked in a big breath of air as he pushed inside.

"Christ," he whispered. "Jesus Christ."

Acting on instinct, Kassidy moved closer to Chris, rubbing his back. He made more sounds, wordless sounds that could have been pain, or maybe were ecstasy.

"Fuck," Dag whispered again. "Tight. So fuckin' tight." He began to move. Kassidy watched as his shaft slid in and out of Chris, amazed at the beauty of it. She leaned down to kiss Chris's shoulder as Dag clasped his hips, picking up his pace. "Not gonna last," he gasped. "Close…Jesus…fuck…"

He yanked Chris's hips higher and Chris pushed back into his strokes, sliding a hand down between his legs to find his cock. "Fuck, me too," he mumbled. "Oh…there it is… goddamn." His body shuddered through his orgasm and then Dag came too, his face taut, hands gripping Chris's hips. Kassidy continued to watch in awe and excitement, her chest full of emotion, absorbing every tremor of Chris's body, listening to his growls of pleasure.

She pressed her cheek to his shoulder. "I love you," she whispered.

His body heaved—his skin was damp against hers—and he let out a groan. "Love you too, Kass. And Dag. Love you."

"Fuck, man." Dag's voice was hoarse. "Love you too."

Kassidy's nose stung and liquid gathered in the corners of her eyes. She pressed another kiss to Chris's shoulder.

"Sweetheart," he murmured. "Gotta look after you too."

She smiled and slid her fingers through his sweat-dampened hair. "I know."

His body shook with silent laughter. The bed bounced as Dag fell down on the other side of Chris. He set his hand on Chris's back again, and Kassidy covered it with her own. They lay there for a while like that, then Kassidy rolled to her back and slid a hand down to her aching pussy. God, she needed to come. Her breasts felt swollen and heavy, and she pulsed against her own palm.

With slow strokes she circled her clit, slicking up her arousal. *Mmmm.*

"Kass," Chris muttered. "Wait."

"It's okay." She languidly stroked herself.

Dag knifed up off the bed and with fast, sure moves had her centered beneath him, his big hands pressing her thighs apart then sliding beneath her butt to lift her pussy to his face. "Gonna eat you," he muttered. "Taste that sweet pussy." He licked at her. "Kass, babe, you're so fucking wet."

"I know," she moaned, shivering in delight at the touch of his tongue on her sensitive flesh. "I know. I'm aching. Watching you guys…that was so beautiful. And so hot."

"Turns you on," he muttered.

"Oh yeah."

Chris shifted beside her and caressed her breasts. She arched her back into his touch, sensation cascading over her body, and when he leaned down to suck a nipple, her womb spasmed. Her hips pushed up into Dag's mouth and she felt his smile there.

"So hot, baby," he whispered, then licked her again, up and down, nibbling at her pussy lips, sucking gently. His tongue circled her clit, and then he went all in, burying his face in her cunt and eating at her hungrily.

"Oh God!" With Chris sucking her nipples and Dag on her clit, and already being so worked up, Kassidy came in fast, hard, almost unbearable waves of pleasure. "Oh my God." She clutched Chris's head to her chest, trembling from her shoulders to her toes.

Dag kissed one inner thigh, then the other, then lowered

her butt to the mattress. He crawled up over her on hands and knees. Chris shifted and Dag leaned to give first him a kiss, then her, soft and lingering and tasting of her own essence.

"Wow," she murmured. "Thanks."

Both guys laughed softly. Dag moved to her side, placing her in the middle, just where she liked to be. It felt so...right.

"I just have one question," she mumbled.

"What's that, babe?" Dag stroked the hair off her face.

"Who's gonna clean up the mess on this comforter?"

Chapter Four

BOTH GUYS BURST OUT LAUGHING. "ISN'T THAT WOMAN'S work?" Dag asked.

She gave a lethargic smile. "I know you're kidding. Otherwise I'd punch you."

"I'll take care of it tomorrow," Dag said. "Since I'm unemployed."

Chris snorted. "Yeah, right."

"Thank you," Kassidy said primly to Dag. "Also, there are dishes to do in the kitchen."

Dag gave her a fast, hard kiss, smiling as he did so.

"Can we get under the covers?" she asked.

"It's too early for bed," Chris grumbled as they all shifted around, tossing the comforter into a corner of the room.

"Okay," Kassidy said, settling in between her men under the sheet. "Then we can talk now."

Chris groaned.

"Chris. You know we have to."

"I know, I know."

"Tell me about Hailey," Dag said softly, rolling to lie on his side and face her. He stroked her arm.

"Okay. Hailey." Kassidy sighed. "Well. After I left you at the hotel on Sunday, I went to her place. I was so confused about everything. So I talked to her about it. She was actually really great. She wasn't judging me. And she even admitted that she'd been jealous of me. Me and Chris, because we seemed to have such a perfect relationship."

"What do you mean *seemed* to have?" Chris demanded.

"Nobody has a perfect relationship," she reminded him with a little smile. "You can be a little stubborn, and there are times I have to remind you that the people who work for you are actually people, with lives and feelings."

He gave her a tight-lipped look. "Yeah, yeah," he said. Then he smiled. "Thanks for reminding me of that."

"Anyway. She also said it was hard to be my sister because I'm so perfect."

"Sweetheart," Chris said, "you're not perfect either."

Kassidy laughed. "I know that! But the whole conversation just showed me that what other people see isn't necessarily the reality. *I* was jealous of *her*...for how much fun she always had, all the boyfriends she had, how easy it was for her to make friends. How she didn't worry about being good or perfect.

"It made me wonder why we compare ourselves to others. We should be happy with what we've got. I always thought she was deriding our relationship, that she thought it was boring that we were so settled down with each other, that we both have steady, corporate jobs. But it turns out she was jealous of that. Then I felt bad that I never knew that, and maybe sometimes when I was defending us to her, I was really just rubbing her nose in it all. But she kind of did the same. I don't know if she knew I was jealous of her, but sometimes it felt like she was showing off how bad she could be and making me feel like a loser good girl."

"Wow," Dag said. "Sibling rivalry lasts right into adulthood."

"I guess it does," Kassidy admitted. "I feel kind of ashamed of that. Jeez, we're adults."

"I get it though," Dag said slowly. "Not the sibling rivalry, but I get how she felt. I lived like that too. Got into trouble, got a reputation, got pissed because nobody could see past that, so I spent my life living up to my own reputation."

Kassidy lifted a hand and touched his whisker-stubbled cheek. "Yeah," she said softly. "Like that. Anyway, it opened my eyes a bit. I'm going to talk to Hailey and maybe we can be better friends."

"That's great, sweetheart," Chris said. "But what about her...um...porn career?"

Ugh. Kassidy's stomach tightened. "Yeah. What about that? Well. I guess I should give her the same respect she gave me and not judge her for doing it. I don't know all her reasons for doing it and maybe I never will understand it, but it's her life."

"Uh-huh." Dag shifted closer. "That's true."

"I only worry about my parents," Kassidy whispered. "I think it might really hurt them if they found out."

"I get that," Dag said. "But you can't take that on yourself, right? If they find out—and it won't be from you—that'll be between them and Hailey."

"True. But still...it would be awful."

"Maybe they'd have the same attitude as you do," Chris suggested. "And not judge her."

Kassidy snorted. "Well, maybe. It took some thinking for me to get to this point though. You're right, Dag. I'll deal with that if it happens. In the meantime, I'm going to try to work on being a better friend and sister to Hailey."

"We're with you, babe. You know that," Dag murmured.

"Yeah. And thank you. I called Hailey about the party and to let her know that things worked out for us. She's working Friday night, but we're going to have lunch on Saturday, she wants to hear about what happened and what's going on with us." She paused. "Okay, Chris, your turn."

They had to prompt him and pull the details out of him, about what he'd alluded to earlier—why he'd never realized his feelings for Dag—and Kassidy was horrified to hear about his dad beating the crap out of him because he'd caught him fooling around with another boy in some kind of youthful exploration. She didn't know his parents well, since they lived so far away and they'd only met a few times, but she lost a bunch of respect for Mr. Manness on hearing that.

"I don't think I'm gay," Chris finally concluded. "I know you thought I was homophobic, Kass, but I don't think I'm that either."

"I never thought that," she protested, pushing his hair off his forehead.

"Yeah you did."

"No I didn't. Seriously! I just wondered why you weren't completely comfortable around Steve and Ryan." Her gay friend from high school and his partner.

"I was comfortable with them!"

"Uh…no. You weren't."

Chris frowned. "I was fine with them."

"You didn't even realize it," she said. "It's okay, Chris."

He looked like he didn't believe her, still frowning. "Huh. Anyway. I wasn't attracted to other men. I love women."

"Ahem." Kassidy lifted her eyebrows.

Chris and Dag both laughed.

"Yeah, I mean in the past. Now just one woman. But there was always something between you and me, Dag...something I didn't want to acknowledge or analyze. And, honestly, I had no idea how you felt. Some kind of deep denial bullshit, I guess." He shook his head. "Don't know how else to make sense of it."

"Maybe you don't have to make sense of it," Dag suggested. "Maybe you just accept it and go with it."

Kassidy looked at Dag and nodded, then looked at Chris, who nodded slowly too. "Yeah," he said. "Okay."

"Good advice for all of us," she murmured. "If I think too much about this, I could start freaking out. And...we don't need to label it, whatever you guys are. Gay. Bi. Whatever. Hailey said she knows people who are attracted to certain people and it doesn't matter if they're male or female, there's just some kind of chemistry between them."

"Yeah," Dag said slowly. "That's it. Totally." He paused. "What else is on the agenda?"

Chris smiled and Kassidy giggled and gave him a little nudge with her head at Dag's teasing question. "The party Friday night," she said. "All our friends are coming over. Obviously we have to tell them Dag's living here with us. Is that how we leave it?"

They all exchanged glances.

"You know I don't give a shit what people think," Dag said quietly. "But I'll go with whatever you two want."

Chris swallowed. "I'm not sure I'm ready to make a big announcement."

"I get that, man. I do."

Kassidy nodded. "Me too. If people suspect something between Dag and me, whatever." She waved a hand. "I vote for letting things settle and develop between us before we go public."

"Done," Dag said immediately.

She let out a long breath. There were going to be many more moments like this. They all knew it. But at least they were all together in it, and with her two guys at her back, she felt like she could handle pretty much anything.

Thursday night, Dag and Kassidy took Chris out for dinner for his birthday, just the three of them, and then went home to give him his gifts. They just got home when Kassidy's parents called to wish Chris a happy birthday, which was nice. Mom was all apologetic about not getting Chris's gift to him, and he assured her that she had enough on her plate, recovering from the car accident. Her doctor's appointment that week had been good news, and she was feeling better and better.

Then Chris's parents called to wish him a happy birthday. Dag and Kassidy listened to him chat with them. They knew he wasn't going to say anything to them about their living arrangement, obviously, and since they lived in Miami it was unlikely they'd be visiting any time soon to see for themselves.

Except they were wrong.

Chris got a funny look on his face. "Seriously?" he said. "When?"

He listened. Dag and Kassidy exchanged glances.

"No, that's great, sure. Uh…with us?" His eyes went wide and now he looked at both of them with a somewhat panicked expression. "Uh…" Clearly he had no idea what to say.

Kassidy read into this that his parents wanted to come visit. Holy shit.

"A hotel might be nice too," he said. "Somewhere nice… downtown… Mom likes to shop…" Then he closed his eyes. "Yeah. Okay. Great. Let me know when your flight gets in."

He hung up and slumped back into the couch. "Jesus fucking Christ. They're coming to visit."

Dag's eyes met Kassidy's again. Uh...*yeah*. Jesus fucking Christ was right.

"They want to stay with us," she guessed.

"Yep. Want to see the new condo. I told them we had three bedrooms so they think there's lots of room."

"There is," Dag said quietly. He laid a hand on Chris's shoulder. "I'll leave."

"Fuck no."

"When are they coming?" Kassidy asked.

"Next weekend."

"Okay." She sucked in a breath and smiled. "We've got lots of time to figure it out. Now, here's your present from me." She had no idea what they were going to do about this, but they'd deal with it.

She hadn't actually bought Chris his gift, but gave him a picture of it inside a birthday card—the office furniture he wanted from IKEA. They'd looked at it for the room that was going to be his office, but hadn't gotten around to buying it.

He leaned over to kiss her, eyes warm. He cupped her jaw. "Thanks, sweetheart."

"We can go pick it up this weekend," she said. "And then you two men can spend the rest of the weekend building it."

Chris grinned. He didn't mind doing stuff like that.

"Build IKEA furniture?" Dag asked. He sat on the other side of Chris on their couch, holding a glass of expensive Shiraz he'd picked up that day. "How domesticated."

"Deal with it, buddy," Chris muttered. "You *are* becoming domesticated."

Dag grinned.

Then Chris opened Dag's present, a small wrapped box.

The gift brought tears to Kassidy's eyes, and Dag and Chris almost too. It was a pendant—a short silver chain in a chunky interlocking style with a silver charm on it, round, with a swirling design. There was a little card about the designer which said the charm was called Trilogy, to signify the intertwining of the heart, mind and spirit.

"But I think it symbolizes the intertwining of *three* hearts, minds and spirits," Dag explained, watching Chris stare at the gift.

Oh my God. Oh my God. Her heart squeezed so hard it hurt, stealing her breath. Chris kept his head bent, no doubt to hide the emotions on his face, and nodded. She laid a hand on his.

"Too soon?" Dag asked, not getting any response. "No worries if it is. And I know you don't wear a lot of jewelry, so, you know, it's cool if you don't wear it."

She looked at Dag and blinked hard at the moisture gathering in her eyes. He leaned back in the corner of the couch in a relaxed pose, holding his glass of red wine, but the faint tightness at the corners of his eyes and mouth revealed his tension.

She swallowed through a constricted throat. It was true, Chris didn't wear a lot of jewelry. But this was sturdy and masculine and beautiful. And meaningful.

Chris cleared his throat and picked it up from the glossy black box it sat in. He unfastened it and lifted it around his neck. It took a few seconds to get the clasp done up again and Kassidy shifted behind him to help.

"There," she whispered.

He laid his fingers flat over the charm and met Dag's eyes. "It's great," he said, voice gruff. "Thanks."

The skin around Dag's eyes softened and the corners of his mouth lifted. "You're welcome."

And then Chris leaned over and kissed Dag, just as he'd kissed Kassidy in thanks for her gift.

She swallowed again, but now smiling. "Okay," she said. "Enough smoochy stuff. Now we have something really important to discuss."

The two guys looked at her.

"What?" Chris asked.

"Everything okay, babe?" Dag added.

"No, it is not. You all are not living in a frat house. If I see one more gob of toothpaste or beard whisker in the sink, I'm gonna lose my shit. Tomorrow, we're going to do a tutorial on how to properly clean the sink."

Dag grinned. "I'll watch your tutorial," he said, "if you promise to do it naked."

Kassidy giggled, losing her stern attitude. "Sure, I'll do it naked," she agreed. "If it'll help to do it naked, I'll even show you how to change the toilet paper roll. It's not difficult." She patted Dag's arm. "You can do it."

The next night they had the party. Dag took care of almost everything. Kassidy had to do some cleaning though, because they'd already established that Chris and Dag's standards when it came to cleanliness in the kitchen and bathrooms weren't at quite the same level as hers.

Anyway, Dag had arranged an extremely cool cocktail party with hot and cold finger foods delivered, cases of booze arranged by the bartender, who brought his own portable bar, glasses and garnishes like lemon and lime slices and celery sticks. He was a smiley, charming guy who said he couldn't make *every* drink someone might order, but pretty damn close. He was so friendly and everyone loved him so much it felt like he was one of their friends, and his tip bowl was overflowing by the end of the evening, which was as it should be.

Dag even arranged the music, his iPod hooked up to their speakers, playing some recognizable popular songs, and some less familiar but great indie songs. The only thing he didn't do was decorate, but, really, who needed a bunch of cheesy *BIG 3-0* decorations?

Their friends provided enough of that with the cards and gifts they brought, like the one that said Chris wasn't *30* he was *XXX*. Everyone laughed, but Chris and Dag and Kassidy exchanged insider glances of amusement at that one. Jeff and Sarah gave him some golf balls that said *New Balls for an Old Body*, and Cole and Tyra had wrapped up a big package of Depends for him. His buddy Matt gave him a bottle of what was supposed to be Viagra, which brought forth another round of hilarity.

"This drug works by increasing blood flow to the penis," Chris read, grinning. "Sexual activity may put extra strain on your heart. If you have severe dizziness, fainting, chest, jaw or left arm pain while having sex, stop and get medical help right away." He looked up. "I do actually get dizzy when I have a hard-on, but that's just because my dick is so big it drains all the blood from the rest of my body."

The others roared with laughter and the guys hooted with derision. Kassidy met Dag's eyes and they shared a private smile.

"In your dreams," Matt called.

"Hey," Jeff said. "What do you get when you cross an owl and a rooster?" After a beat of expectant silence, he answered, "A cock that stays up all night long."

The laughter this time was accompanied by groans.

"This stuff comes with a warning," Chris added. "If you have a painful or prolonged erection lasting four or more hours, stop using this drug and get medical help right away."

"Fuck," Brandon said. "If I had an erection that lasted four hours, I'd call you all and brag about it."

"I had one that lasted all through tenth grade," Jeff said.

Sarah laughed along with everyone else and gave his

shoulder a shove. "If you had an erection that lasted longer than four hours, it would be *me* who needed medical attention."

On top of the joke gifts, though, a bunch of their friends went in together and signed Chris up for a Beer of the Month Club where he'd get different craft beers delivered every month.

"That is pretty damn cool," he said, reading the pamphlet they gave him. "Thanks."

Kassidy's friend Danielle was there and meeting Dag for the first time, since she'd been away traveling in Europe for the first part of her summer vacation. She was a teacher and spent part of every summer traveling.

"Holy hell, Kass," she whispered after she'd been introduced. "He is *hawt*."

Kassidy laughed. "Yep."

"And single…right?"

Kassidy gazed at her friend, her stomach dropping. Okay, awkward moment number one. Shit. "Uh…yeah."

Danielle's eyes brightened and she clutched her mojito. "Excellent."

Kassidy didn't want Danielle making a play for Dag. He was hers. Hers and Chris's. But what was she supposed to say? She nibbled her bottom lip as she watched Danielle bop her way across the room to the bouncy rhythm of Daft Punk singing "Get Lucky", over to Dag's side and commenced flirting with him. Danielle was a cute little blonde and good at flirting.

Danielle was her best girlfriend. Kassidy should tell her. She and Dag and Chris might agree to not tell the others, but Danielle should know. But did Kassidy need to get Chris and Dag to agree to it before sharing that with Danielle?

Shit.

Also, it wasn't fair to put Dag in that position, a girl coming on to him that he had to deal with. And how many times could that happen before people started wondering why he kept pushing away girls?

Dag, however, was a natural-born flirt, and clearly very experienced at this, and he smiled and charmed Danielle without leading her on. Funny, Kassidy never felt jealous of Dag being with Chris, but she felt a little twinge now watching him flirt with Danielle. Stupid. She remembered his first night back when they'd gone out to Kiss, the girls who'd surrounded him all night. But he'd ended up back at their place, with her and Chris. And that was how it would go tonight too. She needed to remember that.

She looked over at Chris, talking to Brandon and Matt and Cole, watched him throw back his head and laugh at something, and caught the faint flash of silver at his throat. He was wearing Dag's chain. And he was having a great time with their friends. Her heart expanded with warmth. Yeah, there were going to be awkward moments. She just hoped they could get through them all.

Chapter Five

THE PARTY WENT LATE FRIDAY NIGHT SINCE THEIR FRIENDS refused to leave until nearly three in the morning, which meant they slept until noon. Kassidy had to jump out of bed and race to get ready to meet Hailey for lunch at Circe, a little bistro not far away. It had a cute patio and she'd envisioned them sitting out there, but the day was overcast and drizzly, so they sat inside.

"How was the party last night?" Hailey asked as the server poured them coffee.

Kassidy grabbed her cup gratefully, still a little groggy and maybe a tiny bit hungover. "It was great. We had so much fun. We'll have another one for Dag, since he turns thirty in a few weeks, and maybe you can come."

"Give me a little more notice than four days."

"Yeah. Sorry about that. I'd completely lost track of when Chris's birthday was. Things were a little, uh…crazy."

"No shit," Hailey said dryly.

Kassidy picked up a menu. She hadn't even had breakfast and it was one o'clock. She settled on a broccoli frittata and

Hailey ordered a spinach salad. When the server left, Hailey eyed her across the small oak table. "So? Give me all the gory details. Last time I saw you, you were sobbing and heartbroken. Now you look…well, actually you look kind of hungover."

"Gee, thanks."

Hailey grinned. "But happy."

Kassidy sighed and smiled. "You're right on both counts. Few too many margaritas last night, and stayed up waaaaay too late. But yeah…" she met her sister's eyes, "…I'm happy."

"Dag's still here."

"Yes." Kassidy filled her in on what had happened.

Hailey listened, mostly without comment, just a few nods and "Oh wow" and "Really?" comments. When Kassidy got to the part about Chris's feelings for Dag, Hailey sat back in her chair wide-eyed and said, "No shit. Seriously?"

"You're the only one we're telling right now," Kassidy said, leaning forward. "This is all new to us too. I wanted you to know. After we talked that night, you knew most of it anyway."

"You're still not telling Mom and Dad."

"No." Their eyes met. "We talked about it and we will tell them, but Hailey…I would never tell them about you."

"I know." Hailey pressed her lips together. "I won't tell them about you either. But…I have to admit…it really is two different things."

"Uh…*yeah*." Kassidy wasn't sure which would be more shocking for their parents, but it was definitely different. "We're going to have to tell them…at some point. We thought we'd let them get to know Dag better, accept that he's living with us, and then when we break the news that we're all in a poly relationship, hopefully they'll already love him."

"Huh. That's optimistic."

Kassidy bit her lip. "You think so?"

"They *are* going to be shocked, Kass, no matter what. Especially because it's you. If it were me…they'd just roll their eyes."

Kassidy sat back in her chair and sipped her coffee. "We need to talk about that."

"About what?"

"About why that is. Why you can get away with all kinds of stuff, but if I do it they'll be shocked."

"Kassidy. You're the good one. You've always been the good one."

Kassidy gazed at her sister. "Can we not talk like that?"

Hailey frowned. "Like what?"

"Like…using labels. Like me being the 'good one' and you the 'bad girl'. That doesn't help anything. And let's not talk about all the ways I've felt wronged by you, or you by me. Let's not list our grievances. That's not going to help. I…I want things to change between us."

Hailey stared at her, holding her own cup of coffee aloft. She blinked. "Oookay. But…" she dropped her gaze, "…I'm not sure I know how to do that."

Kassidy sucked briefly on her bottom lip. "The thing I realized when we talked that night is that we don't know how things look through each other's eyes, or how things feel for each other. You said you were jealous of me because I had Chris and he loved me. But I always felt like you mocked us because we were boring."

Hailey opened her mouth to say something and Kassidy held up a hand. "Just let me finish. That was how it came across to me, even if that wasn't your intention. I'm just sharing that. And I always felt jealous of you, with your wild and carefree lifestyle, all the guys you attracted so easily."

Hailey's eyes widened.

Kassidy took a breath. This was hard. Making yourself so vulnerable to someone who could hurt you. Scary.

"I know you felt you couldn't compete with me for Mom and Dad's attention, because I got good marks and won awards. So you went the other way and tried to be bad, but...I felt the same. I couldn't attract boys like you did. I didn't get invited to all the parties like you did, so I stayed home and studied. But sometimes I hated staying home and studying on a Saturday night."

Hailey's eyes softened. "I see what you're saying."

Kassidy nodded. Her insides tightened but she wanted to do this. "Dag told me that you can choose your friends, and choose who to love. And that's true. If you have a friend who makes you feel inadequate, you can dump them. But you can't just dump your family. You're always going to be there—Christmas, Thanksgiving, anniversaries—I want to be friends with you, Hailey. You're my sister. So let's try to make it better."

After a short pause, Hailey said, "Okay."

Kassidy sucked in a breath through her nose, not sure where to go next. "So. There are things I admire about you. Like I said, the way you attract guys, the way it's so easy for you to flirt and have fun with them. I actually admire the fact that you're happy doing the job you do—the bartending, I mean," she added hastily. "Yeah, I was probably kind of judgy in the past, thinking you could do better, but if you're happy with it, that's what's important."

"Okay," Hailey said, lifting her chin. "Let me tell you about my career. I don't consider myself a bartender. I consider myself a mixologist."

Kassidy blinked.

"And I'm actually the head bartender at Kiss now. Which is one of the hottest nightclubs in Chicago. Also, there aren't that many women head bartenders. I've taken a lot of courses, including some business courses. I've created new cocktails that we've added to the menu at Kiss, and they've actually been reviewed by some food magazines and blogs, and have gotten great reviews."

Kassidy blinked again. Holy crap.

"I entered a competition in New York next month for female mixologists," Hailey continued. "And I'm tossing around the idea of starting my own mixology consulting business."

Kassidy's forehead tightened. "Uh...what would you do?"

"I'd act as a consultant to bars and restaurants and hotels to improve their cocktail list. Also, help them improve their bartenders' knowledge, and how their bar is set up. Every time I go to another bar, I look at things like that and analyze it, and there are a lot of places that could do better." Hailey's eyes met Kassidy's, and the passion in her voice gave Kassidy a warm, soft feeling in her chest.

"Wow, Hailey. I'm sorry I didn't know all that."

"It's just an idea," she said with a shrug. "Do you think it's crazy?"

"It doesn't sound crazy, but I had no idea there was even a demand for something like that."

"I'm not sure there is, which is why it might be crazy. But I have a lot of connections in the business, and I think I'm pretty well-respected." She started talking more about her vision. "It's not only about the drinks on the menu, making sure the menu is balanced and seasonal, but also the type of clientele they have, the location—that makes a difference, whether your menu can support funky new drinks or if you should stay with the classics. I'd build the list, do training for the staff and then maybe have a launch party. That would be good for business. Then I'd do more sales analysis later on to see what's working and what's not."

"Wow," Kassidy said again. "I feel like shit that I didn't know this stuff about you, Hailey."

Hailey's smile was crooked. "Well. I never told you. But… thanks for being interested."

"So." Kassidy looked down. "What about that porn movie you starred in?"

After Kassidy hurtled out of the bed, leaving Dag and Chris alone, Dag lay on his belly, one arm up under the pillow. He listened to Kassidy crashing around in the bathroom getting ready to go, then muttering as she dressed. He lifted his head to peer at her in the dim bedroom, the blinds shutting out most of the morning light. "You okay, babe?"

"Yeah, just running late," she hissed. "Where are my flip-flops, for fuck's sake?"

He smiled into the pillow. Her language got worse when she was stressed. Cute.

Moments later, he heard the outside door close and quiet settled back over the condo.

Dag reached out a hand and found Chris, clasping a hand over his bare shoulder, warm and strong. "You awake, man?" he murmured.

Silence.

Jesus. How had he slept through all that female ruckus?

He let his hand move over Chris's smooth skin, down his back, then up. They were alone. In bed. Naked. For the first time ever.

Then Chris shifted, slowly rolling to his back. "What time is it?" he mumbled.

"Not sure. Noon. Past noon."

"Shit. Slept in."

"Yeah. Late night." Dag's hand now found Chris's hard chest.

"We gotta get going." Chris threw back the covers and jumped out of bed. "Got shit to do today."

Dag's hand dropped to the mattress as Chris disappeared into the bathroom. He heard the toilet flush, then the shower start. He lay there, heaviness seeping through his body. Letting out a long breath, he rolled to his back and stared at the ceiling.

Okay. They had shit to do today. No lazing around in bed on a Saturday for a little fucking around. Just the two of them. Ah well. This might take a while.

He rolled out of the bed and ambled to the kitchen, completely naked. As he opened the door, the fridge blasted him with enough cold to shrink his dick, which was saying something considering the epic morning wood he was displaying. He grabbed a can of Coke, popped the top and drank deeply.

He wiped a hand across the back of his mouth and sauntered back into the living room. For a moment he considered joining Chris in the shower. His dick rebounded and practically led him there, thinking of a slick, wet, naked Chris soaping up in the shower. Christ, he could picture the rounded muscles of his biceps flexing, covered with bubbles as he washed himself. He pictured Chris's hands on his dick and balls, washing there, stroking himself...fuck, he was hard as a table leg again.

He started toward the bedroom, Coke can gripped in his hand, but the shower stopped.

Fuck.

He sat on the bed, drinking his Coke, waiting for Chris to emerge. When he did, he had a towel around his hips, and the sight of that body made need explode inside Dag and sweat break out on his forehead. His cock was a throbbing spike.

"Dude," he said casually, leaning on one hand. "What's the rush?"

Chris glanced at him. His gaze ran up and down over Dag's

naked body, pausing on his enormous erection. He continued over to the dresser and yanked open a drawer. "No rush." He shrugged. "I wanna get to IKEA and get that furniture. It'll take a while to put it together."

"Isn't Kassidy going to come with us?"

Chris turned to him with a grin, even as he dropped the towel and pulled on a pair of boxers. Dag's cock twitched. He watched Chris adjust the elastic around his hips with his thumbs hooked beneath it, so masculine, so fucking hot. "No way, man. We take her into that store and we'll be there for fucking hours. Seriously."

"Huh." Dag could see this.

"She'll want to look at every damn thing," Chris continued, stepping into a pair of knee-length plaid shorts. He flicked up the fly and did up the button. Dag continued to watch his movements with heated interest. "You name it. Then she'll want to completely redecorate. I'm not kidding."

"Yeah." Dag drained the Coke. "I get it."

"If we just go, we can be in and out faster than you can say 'Allen wrench'."

Dag laughed. "Okay. Let's do it."

Whatever. It was domesticated and tame. It wasn't rolling around hot and sweaty on rumpled sheets. But it was with Chris.

As they pulled onto the ramp for I-90, Chris driving, Dag in the passenger seat, Dag said, "So. Wanna talk?"

Chris slid him a sideways glance. "About what?"

"Sex."

Chris choked. "What?"

Dag grinned. "Sex. Between you and me."

"Jesus."

"I know you were thinking about it. Not as in horny

thinking about it—well, okay, maybe that too—I mean, it's understandable that you might have questions."

Chris swallowed.

"So talk to me."

Silence.

Dag repressed a sigh. "I know you like to be in control. Are you worried that because you bottomed for me you're less dominant?"

"Jesus Christ." Chris pressed his lips together, staring out the windshield. "Okay, yeah, I thought about that."

"It doesn't necessarily mean that," Dag added, glad Chris had finally opened up, even just a bit. "Just so you know, I like to switch things up. Everyone has their own preferences, and you need to experiment and try things out to know what you like. So, if you want to top, I'm into that. Big-time."

Chris's Adam's apple rose and fell again.

"Okay," he muttered. "Good to know."

"So...you wanna try that?"

Chris lifted his chin. "Yeah."

"It's all about what feels good. You gotta tell me, babe. It's gotta be good for both of us, no matter how we do it."

"Right. Fuck. I can't believe we're talking about this."

Dag reached over and gave Chris's thigh a hard squeeze. "We have to talk. I'm gonna make you, even when you don't want to."

Chris shot him another sidelong glance, and his lips twitched. "Okay."

They bought the furniture, loaded it into Chris's vehicle, and unloaded it and carried it into the condo, which was a bit of a workout, reminding Dag that he should look into a gym membership if he was going to stay in Chicago. They also made two stops on the way home—one at a drugstore for a huge bottle of lube, which made Chris shake his head and flush, the other stop for sub sandwiches for lunch. They ate them as they contemplated the gazillion pieces of furniture they now had to assemble.

"Shit," Dag said. "This could take a while."

"Yeah."

"Can't you buy this stuff already built?"

"Sure, but you have to pay extra."

Dag resisted the urge to roll his eyes. It would totally be worth it, but then, he wasn't the one paying for this stuff, Kassidy was. "If I'd known this, I would have paid for it."

Chris gave him a sharp look. "Yeah, there you go again with the money thing."

"Jesus Christ. So I have money? What the hell is wrong with that?"

"Nothing." Chris scowled. "I don't know why it bugs me. I have money, okay? I make well over six figures a year, plus bonuses. You don't need to help us out."

"I'm not 'helping you out'. Christ. It'd be worth it to me to have more time with you two, instead of spending the whole fucking weekend building furniture."

"Come on, it's fun."

"Seriously?"

"Yeah. I like building stuff, putting shit together." He narrowed his eyes at Dag. "You don't have to help if you have better things to do."

Dag shook his head, crumpling up the paper wrapper of his sandwich. "I could probably think of twenty better things to do, but, shit, man." He reached for the printed instructions, then muttered, "Whatever." He wanted to be with Chris, but didn't want to sound all sappy.

Chris was organized and methodical, different than Dag

who would've just jumped in. Chris cleared working space, figured out what they needed, and then got to work, giving Dag directions. Yeah, he was the boss. Dag smiled. He'd let him take charge this time. But not every time…

Kassidy arrived home a while later from her lunch with Hailey. She stood in the door, surveying them sitting on the floor with pieces all around them. "Hey," she said. "You went without me?"

Chris and Dag's eyes met and a glimmer of amusement passed between them.

"Yeah, didn't know how long you'd be," Chris said. "I wanted to get started."

"Damn." Her bottom lip pushed out. "I haven't been to IKEA in ages. I wanted to look at kitchen stuff."

"We don't need any more kitchen stuff," Chris replied.

"You did that on purpose," Kassidy said. But she was smiling.

Chris smiled back at her. "Yeah."

She rolled her eyes.

"How'd lunch go?" Dag asked.

"Pretty good." She crossed her arms and leaned against the doorframe. "I learned stuff about my sister I never knew." She told them about Hailey's mixology ambitions. "I'm kind of ashamed I didn't know that stuff about her. But we had a good talk. It's a start, I hope."

"Did you ask her why she made a porn movie?"

"Yeah," she said slowly. "That was something I didn't want to talk about at first, but I forced myself to ask. I think she feels it was a mistake. She did it because some guy came into Kiss one night and was flirting with her and telling her how gorgeous and sexy she was and would she want to be in a movie…typical lines…and it was true, but turned out to be a porn movie. She said she didn't see anything wrong with it, it was good money, but I suspect it was just another way to be as bad as she could be, to shock people."

Kassidy shook her head. "She doesn't have to do that. Maybe…I don't know, maybe now that I've told her I'm impressed with what she's doing with her career, she won't feel a need to be so outrageous. Or maybe it has nothing to do with me, and I'm just clueless and naive."

"Babe," Dag said. "You're sweet. Not naive. And definitely not clueless. I think you've got a good read on her."

"You're always good at dealing with people," Chris muttered. "Hailey's wacked but still…"

"She's my sister."

"Yeah."

"You know," Kassidy said. "We could've paid to get this stuff built and delivered."

Dag choked on a laugh and met Chris's eyes. "Great idea," he said.

Chris shook his head and laughed.

At least Chris didn't take himself that seriously; he could still take a joke. A hot sensation swelled in Dag's chest. Love.

Chapter Six

As they ate dinner that night—tacos Kassidy made—Dag said, "So what are we going to do about your parents coming to visit, Chris?"

Chris's gut clenched and he looked down at the soft tortilla in his hand. "Fuck if I know," he muttered. "Shit. Why now?"

For a moment they all went silent, thinking about this problem. Chris shook his head. He loved his parents but, man, this was bad timing. He was happy to have them visit, pleased to show off the new condo he and Kassidy had bought, proud to show off how nice Kassidy had made it look. They loved Kassidy. But, wow, his dad would have a stroke if he knew what was going on with Dag.

But was this something he could keep from them forever?

"Like I said," Dag spoke up. "I'll leave if you want. Even if it's just for a few days. I can go stay at the hotel again."

"No." Chris's response was immediate. Then he dropped the taco to his plate and rubbed between his eyes.

"It might be the best solution," Dag continued quietly. "I don't mind. If it makes things easier for you."

Yeah, it might be the best solution. But after everything they'd gone through, Chris found himself not wanting Dag to leave again, even if it was mutually agreed on. Guilt about kicking Dag out last weekend still weighed heavily on him. Guilt about hurting Dag, unintentionally, also bore down on him.

What was the alternative though? He could just picture his parents there, and he and Dag and Kassidy saying good night to them and heading into the bedroom. Together. Yeah, that would go over well.

"Look, this is soon," Dag said. "Don't sweat it that you don't want them to know. You might *never* want them to know."

Chris raised his eyes and looked at Dag. "It's fucking tough, man."

"I know." Dag reached out and grabbed his hand. "I know. Let me do this."

Kassidy watched the two of them, a faint crease between her eyebrows, her pretty mouth tight. "We'll do whatever you want, Chris," she added. "We know your parents wouldn't take it well. That's nothing on you."

"I hate this," Chris said.

Dag's eyes flickered. "Hate what?"

"I hate lying. I hate hiding things. I hate it that I feel I have to." He stared at Dag, whose face softened.

"I know."

"I told you that I would tell them if I was going to see them. Like I said, it's not fair to you to deny your relationship with us. I'm not ashamed of it."

"I know," Dag said softly, holding his gaze.

"It's reality," Kassidy added softly. "We all know that. It doesn't matter, honey. We're together, and we love each other, even if we do have to hide it from some people, in the end it doesn't make any difference to us. Right?"

He nodded, his throat dry and rough. He picked up the beer sitting next to his plate and took a big swallow. "Right. Okay. That's what we'll do. They arrive Saturday. I'll go pick them up at the airport. They're staying for a week."

"Fuck! A whole week?" Dag shook his head.

"Yeah. It sucks."

"Whatever. We'll live through it."

As they ate and talked about more inconsequential things, Chris tried to imagine the future. He'd always known Kassidy would be in his future. He loved her. He was probably going to marry her. They'd probably have kids. But now he couldn't imagine that future without Dag, without him there too, living with them. What if his parents wanted to spend Christmas together? Were they going to ship Dag out to a hotel? Or what if his parents invited them to Miami for Christmas? Would they leave him behind?

He was going to tell his parents.

Maybe.

Next time.

No, he was going to do it this time.

Fuck it, he had no clue what he was going to do. "I need another beer," he announced, pushing back his chair. "Anyone else?"

Kassidy smiled at him and handed him her wineglass, and he carried it to the fridge to refill it and get another beer.

"Let me mull it over," he said as he sat back down.

"Mull what over?" Kassidy asked. "Going for a swim at my parents' tomorrow?"

He blinked at her. "Uh...sorry, I guess I wasn't paying attention. We're going swimming at your parents' tomorrow?"

She grinned. "They invited us. It's supposed to be super hot tomorrow. And you can get your birthday present."

"Huh. Okay. But, uh, I meant, let me mull over what to do about my parents."

"Chris…"

He shook his head. "I have to deal with it some time."

"It doesn't have to be now."

"I know. I just need to figure some shit out in my head."

"Okay. Hey, I got a wedding invitation in the mail today."

"Oh yeah? Who from?"

"My friend Taisha. From college?" She looked at Dag. "She lives in Los Angeles now, but she's coming home to Chicago to get married."

"Cool."

"I knew she was getting married, but I wasn't sure if I'd get an invitation. I didn't know how big the wedding would be." She frowned briefly and bit her lip, then shook her head. "I have to check with Danielle and see if she got one too."

Chris listened to Kassidy go on about wedding gifts and maybe buying a new dress to wear and who would be at the wedding, relaxing a little as he let himself be distracted from thinking about his parents.

"So wild times on a Saturday night," Dag said as they got up from the table. "Building furniture."

Kassidy smiled at him, picking up their plates. "Do you want to go out? We could do that."

He smiled back at her. "Nah. I'm just yanking your chains." He crowded her up against the counter and kissed the side of her neck. Chris watched as her eyes drifted closed and her head tilted. His groin tightened. "This is where I want to be," Dag murmured. His tongue stroked over Kassidy's smooth skin and his mouth closed over her earlobe. "Right…here…"

She gave a soft moan and Dag's pelvis pressed deeper against her ass. Blood sizzled through Chris's veins. Watching them together was so fucking hot.

Dag slid his arms around Kassidy from behind and cupped her breasts. Her soft intake of air matched the leap in Chris's pulse.

"Forget building the furniture," Chris said, his voice coming out rough. "I wanna watch you two fuck."

They both turned to look at him, a smile playing on Dag's lips, Kassidy's eyes warm and heavy lidded. "Right," she whispered. "You like to watch."

"Should we give him a show?" Dag murmured near her ear, loud enough for Chris to hear.

Chris's dick throbbed.

"Okay. But not in the kitchen."

Dag laughed softly and Chris had to smile too. "Living room. On the couch."

Dag stepped back but didn't release Kassidy, turning her and then walking her out of the kitchen. As she passed Chris, she trailed her fingers over his cheek and gave him a wink.

Chris shoved back his chair so fast it almost tipped over, and followed them into the living room. They took the couch and he dropped into an armchair.

"I heard a rumor," Dag said, mouth on her neck, his hands all over her, "that you want to be a bad girl."

She gave a breathy laugh. "Where did you hear such a thing?"

"Hmm." He kissed her throat and gave one of her tits a gentle squeeze. "Doesn't matter. How bad do you want to be, babe?"

"I'm not bad. I'm good."

"You certainly are," Dag agreed and when his tongue traced up the side of Kassidy's neck Chris's blood pumped hot through his veins. He rubbed his aching cock through his shorts. "Good at many things."

Dag's hand slid from her breast down over her stomach and

between her legs. Leaning back into the couch cushions, she parted her thighs with a soft moan. His hand rubbed her there, over her shorts and panties, in a slow, sensual rhythm. He kissed her mouth for long moments, with lots of tongue, then kissed his way over her cheek, jaw and throat. He nudged aside the wide, loose neckline of her T-shirt until it dropped off her shoulder, stroked his tongue over her collarbone and then gave the top curve of her breast an openmouthed kiss.

Kassidy's hand slid into Dag's dark hair, her other arm stretched behind him. She shifted her weight a little and hitched one knee up, bending it, nudging Dag's crotch with it, giving him more access to her pussy and giving Chris a better view. Too bad she still had all those clothes on.

"Fuck, I love watching you two," Chris said hoarsely, pressing his engorged cock. "So fucking hot."

Dag swept Kassidy's T-shirt even lower, pushing the cup of her strapless bra out of the way, flashing Chris a glimpse of creamy breast and small brown nipple. Chris's breathing quickened, his heart drumming as he watched Dag take Kassidy's nipple into his mouth. Eyes closed, Dag's face wore a look of rapture as he pulled the bud into his mouth, sucked on it, released it. His tongue licked over the tight peak, then he suckled it again, and again. Kassidy began to shift on the couch, making needy little noises.

Dag popped open the button of her shorts, tugged down the zipper and slipped his hand inside as he continued to feast on her breast.

"Oh yeah," Kassidy panted. "That's so good. Yes…touch me there."

Chris could imagine how silky and wet her pussy was. Having her nipples sucked made her hot like nothing else. His cock pulsed, now so hard he hurt. He swallowed.

Then Dag halted, pulled his hand free of Kassidy's shorts.

She gave a small cry of displeasure, but Dag was pulling the T-shirt off over her head. "Take off your bra," he ordered her in a low, rough tone. She reached behind her to unfasten it and then it was gone and she was topless, slouched on the couch in little shorts that were open, her long, smooth legs spread. Chris studied her torso, her narrow rib cage, her perfect round breasts. Holy hell.

"Beautiful, Kass," he called to her. "So beautiful."

He wanted to touch her too. Yeah, he liked to watch, but this was becoming painful. With shaky fingers, he unzipped his own shorts, shoving them low on his hips, and pulled out his dick.

"I guess he likes this," Dag said to Kassidy, and she looked at Chris and saw him jacking himself off. Her lips curved and her eyes went dark.

"That's beautiful too," she said, watching him, and, fuck, that was hot. When she swiped her tongue across her bottom lip, he nearly lost it. He had to stop, focus on breathing. He slid his other hand up under his shirt and rubbed his chest, which rose and fell in rapid rhythm.

"It is," Dag agreed. "You'd probably like to suck his dick, wouldn't you?"

"Yes."

"Me too."

Oh Jesus. They were fucking torturing him.

Dag's hand had returned to Kassidy's pussy inside her loose shorts, fingers working her there as he now licked and sucked both nipples, kissing his way across her chest between her breasts. Seeing his tongue on her skin, her nipple between his lips…fuck. Chris couldn't stop the groan that rose in his throat.

He focused in on Kassidy as she started to make her orgasm sounds, the little whimpers he knew so well. Her thighs tightened, her ass lifted off the couch and a pink flush stained her chest and washed up into her cheeks as Dag made her come with his fingers.

"Fucking sweet, Kass," Dag whispered, kissing her mouth again, swallowing those sexy sounds.

He didn't give her time to recover. "Gotta be inside you," he muttered. He stood and stripped his own T-shirt off, shoved down his jeans and kicked them aside. Chris's gaze tracked from Dag's hard chest, down over ridged abs, the thick dark hair at his groin that was so aggressively male and erotic, his long, muscled legs.

Dag grabbed Kassidy's hands and pulled her to standing. Her lips parted with surprise as he yanked her shorts down, turned them both and sat back down with her sitting on his lap, facing Chris.

"Oh," she breathed.

"You can watch each other," Dag decreed, lifting her easily over his cock, then slowly lowering her onto him. Chris watched her face, watched her teeth sink into her bottom lip as Dag stretched and filled her, watched her eyelids grow heavy. She met his eyes and, holy hell, the connection sizzled between them, despite the distance separating them, as Dag's cock impaled her pretty pussy.

Chris's gaze dropped to where she and Dag were joined, her thighs straddling his, the contrast between their legs amazing and enthralling—Dag's dark hair and darker skin against her smooth, lightly tanned flesh, her sleek pussy lips surrounding the thick spear of flesh, Dag's testicles drawn up tight and beautiful at the base.

Chris's hand resumed stroking his own shaft.

"Look at him," Dag said again from behind Kass. "Jacking off. Watching us."

"Yeah." She gave a slow blink, her lips parted, then her eyes drifted closed on a long moan as Dag filled her completely.

"Gonna fuck you," Dag said, lips on Kassidy's shoulder. "Then we'll suck him off. Together. Okay?"

"I thought he just wanted to watch," she protested, lips quirked.

Chris rubbed his nipple and choked out, "Not sure I can last."

"Not gonna take long," Dag growled, and his hands on Kassidy's waist lifted her. Up and down, she began to move on his shaft, her breasts jiggling with every impact. Dag's hips lifted, powering up into her and she met him eagerly, soft cries falling from her lips.

"How does she look, man?" Dag asked Chris. "Gorgeous?"

"So gorgeous." Chris panted. "Tits bouncing, her pussy taking you, your dick all shiny and wet...Jesus."

Now Dag groaned, and Chris liked that his words had excited him too. The sounds of their bodies slapping together, their heavy breathing and whimpers of pleasure filled the room. Dag's fingers tightened on Kassidy's hips, her head fell back and she slipped her hand down to touch herself.

"Fuck," Chris muttered.

"Yeah, babe, that's it. Take it...take another one. Good for you."

"Want it...wanna come..."

Their pace quickened, faster, harder, and then Kassidy gave a long wail, going rigid above Dag. He powered on, once more, twice, then held her tight against him as he too came, his balls contracting visibly.

That was so...fucking...hot.

Chris could hardly breathe, his lungs burned so much. Tingles simmered at the base of his spine, sweat beaded on his forehead. He was so close but, damn, he wanted those mouths on him...

A moment later, they both kneeled in front of him, and he

collapsed back in the chair, letting Kassidy's soft hand circle his cock, Dag's harder fingers caressing his balls. Jesus fucking Christ. Chris closed his eyes and gave himself over to them, to the assault of pleasure on every nerve ending in his body. When Kassidy's mouth closed over the tip of his cock and gently sucked, the top of his head pounded. She traced the crown with her tongue, lapped at him with her tongue, then drew him deep into her mouth again. She bobbed her head up and down a few times, and the friction of her lips on his flesh felt fantastic. Then she lifted off, and another mouth took him in, bigger, harder, no less hot. Dag's tongue was magic too, more aggressive, his hand on Chris's shaft firmer. Christ. Oh Christ.

They took turns greedily licking and sucking him, tonguing his balls, caressing his thighs and he came, too fast. His orgasm roared through him, thundering in his ears, blinding him. Heat exploded in his balls, racing up his spine, down his dick.

Dag's hand on his cock grew slicker with his come, and Chris felt both their mouths hovering there, so close, lapping at him, lapping at each other, kissing each other around his pulsing shaft, their lips wet.

His chest heaved, his thighs quivered and the roaring in his ears gradually receded. Spent. He was spent. He couldn't even lift his arms. He struggled to open his eyes just as Kassidy crawled up into the big chair with him, curling onto his lap, hand on the side of his neck, head on his shoulder. Dag's weight settled onto the arm of the chair and he leaned in to press a kiss to Chris's forehead.

"Fuck, man," Dag said. "That was amazing."

"Yeah," Chris wheezed, finding Kassidy's hip with one hand. "Fucking amazing. Love you both."

"Mmm." Kassidy kissed his throat. "I love you both too. You give me so much."

"Please tell me we don't have to go build office furniture now," Dag growled.

Chris choked on a laugh. "Yeah...no." He managed to get his other hand up to squeeze Dag's thigh. "Can't get enough of you...both of you. Just wanna get into bed and do that all over again."

"I think we could switch it up a little," Dag suggested. "You sure you're up for it?"

"Uh...not at the moment." Chris gave a pointed look at his crotch. "But I will be."

"Still got that Viagra? 'Cause you're gonna need it, buddy."

Kassidy's body shook with giggles against his, and he wrapped his arm around her and squeezed.

Chapter Seven

"IT'S PRETTY FUCKING HARD," DAG GROWLED IN A LOW VOICE, "to keep my hands off you in that little bikini."

Kassidy smiled, lying on her back on a lounge chair beside her parents' pool, eyes closed against the bright sun. "I thought you were going to say something else is hard," she murmured.

"That too. Goddammit."

Her smile deepened. Yeah, it was hard to keep her hands off him too around her parents. More than once she'd had to stop herself from touching him, even kissing him, as they'd moved around in the kitchen, helping her mom get some snacks together since her mom was still not fully mobile. When the three of them had jumped into the pool, they'd managed to disguise some sexy petting as horsing around, with much laughter and a few screams as Chris and Dag dunked her and tickled her.

She let her fingertips slide over and brush against his thigh on the lounger beside her. He sucked in a breath. "Kass."

She sighed and pulled her hand back.

"You're being quite the risk taker today," he said. "Usually it's me getting in trouble."

"I know you like taking risks," she said. "But I think you've learned when and where to do that. I don't think you could have developed a business and sold it for millions of dollars if you took stupid risks."

"True. And…" He paused.

She lifted her head to look at him. "What?"

"It's easy being reckless when you have nothing to lose."

Their eyes met and emotion climbed up her throat as she got what he meant. She gave him a shaky smile.

Chris hauled himself out of the pool after doing a few laps. "That felt good," he said, panting a little. Kassidy cracked an eye open to watch him grab a towel and start drying off his torso. The water running down his tanned skin, over all those muscles, was delicious.

"This is nice," Kassidy agreed. The warmth of the sun seeped right into her bones, relaxing her. She breathed in the faint scent of chlorine mingled with coconut sunscreen and then let it out on a lengthy exhalation that eased more tension out of her muscles. "So nice to have a pool."

"I always wanted a pool when I was a kid," Dag said. "It seemed like the ultimate luxury. But that was so out of the question…stupid kid's dream."

Kassidy sucked her bottom lip briefly, sympathy washing through her at the crappy childhood he'd had. "Maybe we could…" Then she stopped herself. Her parents were sitting in the shade and probably couldn't hear, but still…she probably shouldn't suggest they buy a new house together, one with a pool.

This was the hard part. Watching what they said. Watching what they did.

But they were doing a good job.

"I need another drink," she murmured.

Both guys jumped up. "I'll get it," Dag said.

"No, I'm going in," Chris said. "What do you want, sweetheart? Another hard lemonade?"

"You're too wet to go in," Dag said. "I'll go. Hard lemonade, got it. Chris? Want something?"

Chris grinned. "Another beer. Thanks, dude."

When Dag had gone, Chris appropriated his lounge chair and stretched out beside Kassidy. Unlike Dag, he didn't have to stop himself from touching her, and he reached out and stroked a hand over her arm and shoulder. "Need more sunscreen?"

"Um, yeah. I want to turn over. Can you do my back?"

"You bet."

She lowered the back of the chair so it was flat and stretched out on her stomach, chin on her hands. Chris squeezed cold lotion onto her hot skin and she squealed. But then his hands massaged it into her and she sighed. And remembered the day she and Chris and Dag had gone to the beach and they'd both rubbed sunscreen on her. And they hadn't given a shit who saw them or what they thought.

That had felt naughty and, yeah, she'd been going for the naughty, but the freedom to be themselves and do what they felt like doing without worrying what anyone thought seemed so enviably easy now.

She sighed.

"Here you go, babe." Dag handed her the hard lemonade.

Babe.

She froze and glanced at her parents, striving to stay casual. Yes, they could hear. "Thanks," she said lightly, sitting up and taking the cold glass.

Dag looked at Chris. "You're in my chair," he said with a chin lift.

"Where's my beer?"

"You're in my chair."

She bugged her eyes out at them to get them to stop.

"Sit over there," Chris said. "Now give me my beer."

Dag shook his head and handed the beer over, then with a huge hard-done-by sigh he sat in the other chair, which was not next to Kassidy.

Luckily, Mom and Dad were just amused by this.

"Do you all want to stay for dinner?" Mom called over. "And don't worry, I'm not cooking. We can order pizza or something."

Kassidy glanced at Chris then Dag to gauge their responses. "Guys?"

"Ah…sure," Chris said.

"Pizza sounds good," Dag added. "I don't suppose you'd let me buy."

Mom laughed. "No."

"It'd be my thanks for letting me hang out with your family and enjoy your pool," he said with a wicked, charming grin.

"Oh heavens," Mom said. "You're a friend of Chris's. Besides, I think we owe you for the times you came and stayed with me when I was bedridden."

Dag had helped out, with Dad and Chris and Kassidy working and not able to take a lot of time off. Kassidy looked at Mom, who was gazing at Dag with a warm softness on her face. She'd fallen a little in love with Dag.

This was good. They wanted her parents to love Dag, to accept him as one of the family. She just wished it could be now.

She sucked back her lemonade.

Dad went inside to order pizza.

Then Chris opened his birthday present, which was a cool little ball speaker that he could plug into his phone or laptop or tablet, and a really nice Rag and Bone T-shirt. They told her parents about the new office furniture and Chris and Dag's epic building adventure that had eventually resulted in success. Dag asked Dad about the work involved in having a pool. Chris told Mom and Dad that his parents were coming next weekend. They'd never met his parents, and Mom was thrilled, only wishing she wasn't still dealing with her pelvic fracture, although she was much, much better.

"We'll have them over for dinner," she said. "You pick the night and we'll make it work."

Chris nodded, his mouth in a glum line.

A while later when Kassidy was helping Mom put the pizza away, just the two of them in the kitchen, Mom said, "Kassie, does Chris not get along with his family?"

Kassidy blinked at her. "Um…why do you ask that?"

"He didn't look very happy that they're coming. Are there problems? You've met them, right?"

"Yes, I've met them. A couple of times. Um…I think Chris and his dad are kind of…not that close. His dad's very conservative. He was really strict with Chris. I mean, they don't hate each other. Just…"

"I understand." She nodded. "So, your condo will be pretty full, with Dag *and* Chris's parents there."

"Oh, Dag's going to go stay in a hotel again while they're here."

Mom tipped her head. "Oh no. Really? Why?"

"Uh…" Crap. Crap crap crap. Her mind scrambled. "We just built all that office furniture in Chris's office, so there's no bed in there."

"Oh, right." Mom grabbed a cloth and wiped the counter. "Dag could stay here if he wants. Cheaper than a hotel."

Kassidy laughed. "He has millions of dollars, Mom. But thank you. That's nice of you to offer."

"Well, maybe he'd rather stay here than in a hotel. More homey. I'm doing more cooking now…"

Jeez, Mom *did* love him. Kassidy shook her head, smiling. "You can ask him."

"He's such a nice boy."

Kassidy gaped at her mom. She'd never heard Dag described that way. Bad boy, yes. Nice boy, hell no.

But, like many bad boys, his surface cockiness and sarcasm hid the real man on the inside—the smart, hard-working, caring guy who'd do anything for people he loved. Kassidy's chest went all hot and soft. "Yeah," she finally said, "he is."

Mom glanced at her. "He really likes you."

That hot softness vanished, replaced with ice. "Um…good. I mean, I hope so. He's Chris's friend, so I want him to like me."

Mom tilted her head and pursed her lips. "I kind of meant…he really *likes* you."

Kassidy stared at Mom, her stomach quivering. "Oh. No no, I don't think so."

Mom shrugged and resumed wiping the counter. "Okay. I just…wouldn't want there to be any problems between you and Chris."

Kassidy sucked in a sharp breath. "Of course not! I love Chris."

"I know you do." She smiled. "And that makes me happy. You know we love Chris too."

Kassidy swallowed. "I know. Thanks, Mom."

The kitchen now spotless, she escaped back outside where the men sat around the outdoor table talking about politics and, amazingly, not arguing. "We should get going," she said brightly. "Chris and I have to work tomorrow."

"Hey," Dag said. "What do you think I do? Lie around and watch soap operas and eat candy all day?"

She had to laugh. "No. You've been busy." He *had* been working hard at his new business.

They gathered up all their stuff—towels, wet swimsuits, sunscreen—and as they walked through the kitchen to leave, Mom called, "Dag…Kassie told me you're moving back to a hotel when Chris's parents are here."

She could have burst out laughing at the look on Chris and Dag's face. They clearly were thinking she'd told her mom why that was.

"You can stay here if you want," she went on. "We have tons of room and this time you won't have to babysit me." She fluttered her eyelashes at him. "I can make you home-cooked meals, and you can do laundry and spread out. It'll be better than a hotel."

"Uh…yeah. I'll…think about that. Definitely. Thank you."

Kassidy sucked on her bottom lip to keep from laughing.

"We have Wi-Fi," Mom added.

Dag grinned. "The magic words."

There were hugs all around, thanks for the pizza and pool time, and then Dag, Chris and Kassidy were in Chris's vehicle heading for home.

"Whoa," she said. "I did not tell my mom anything, but she is *very* perceptive. Like, scary perceptive." She shared her conversation with her mom.

"Shit," Dag said. "I thought I was putting on a pretty good act."

"I thought so too."

They all considered the implications of Mom having rightly read Dag's feelings for Kassidy. *Yikes.*

Kassidy's cell phone rang in her purse and she pulled it out.

"Danielle," she said to the guys after looking at the display. She answered the phone. "Hey, girl."

"Hey! Where are you?"

"On our way home from my parents' place."

"Oh, nice. How's your mom doing?"

"Good. Much better. She's pretty amazing."

"That's great. So listen…do you have Dag's cell phone number?"

Her chin lowered abruptly and her body tightened. "Uh… yeah. Why?"

"I want to call him next week. What do you think? Invite him out for a drink or something to, you know, get to know each other a bit. He's so freakin' hot, Kass!"

Her body tightened even more and her teeth ground together. She did not know what to say to her friend. At lightning speed, she considered her options. Give her Dag's number and let him deal with it. Refuse to give her his number for some made-up reason. Tell her the truth.

She closed her eyes. She knew which it had to be, but she certainly wasn't going to tell her something that monumental over the phone.

"Dani, there's something you need to know…"

"About Dag?"

"Yes."

"Oh Christ. Is he gay?"

She took a deep breath. "Let's have lunch tomorrow. I'll tell you all about it."

She sighed. "Shit. This doesn't sound good. Okay, sure. Where should we go?"

They arranged to meet at a little café not far from Kassidy's office.

"What was that?" Chris asked as soon as she ended the call.

She shifted in her seat to look at Dag in the back. "Danielle has a little crush on you. She wanted me to give her your number so she could call and ask you out."

"Shut the fuck up."

"I'm not kidding."

"You didn't give it to her," he stated unnecessarily.

"No. I didn't. You guys...I have to tell her the truth. She's my best friend. I don't want to make shit up and lie to her to keep her away from Dag."

"I'll deal with her," he said.

"Oh God, Dag." She stared at him, emotion filling her chest. Mom was right. He *was* a nice guy under that bad-boy exterior. He was totally willing to take responsibility and be the bad guy in the scenario, somehow brushing Danielle off. That he would do that for her...for them...God. Her throat got a little thick. Finally she continued, "No. I'll tell her. She loves me. It'll be fine."

"Uh, sweetheart," Chris said, "Danielle likes to gossip."

This was not wrong. She wrinkled her nose. "I know. But I'll make her swear not to tell anyone. You're okay with this, right, guys?"

"Fuck," Chris muttered. "Yeah."

Dag shrugged. "Sure."

"It'll be okay." She smiled and tried to reassure both guys of that, even though she wasn't sure herself.

"So? I was right, wasn't I?" Danielle looked at Kassidy expectantly across the small restaurant table the next day at lunch. "He's gay." She sighed. "All the good ones are. Taken or gay."

Kassidy had to laugh. "Oh, honey. That's not true."

"It is. You know it is. Okay, you don't know, because you found Chris, the last of the heterosexual good ones."

Oh boy. This was going to be tough to explain. "What looks good?" Kassidy asked, picking up her menu.

"I have to have a salad. I gained five pounds in Europe, eating bread and croissants."

"I don't believe you. You look great."

"Aw. Thanks. Okay, Cobb salad."

"You know that's not really low cal, right?"

Danielle's mouth twisted. "Huh. You're right. God, I don't want an egg-white omelet."

"How about the chicken tenders? The sweet chili ones aren't breaded and fried, and they're really good."

Danielle frowned. "That sauce though...yeah, okay. With a tossed salad, dressing on the side, that's not bad."

"I'll have the same. I love that chicken."

Their server approached to take their order, and then they were alone.

"Okay, so about Dag," Kassidy said, looking down at the white tablecloth. Her insides, already in painful knots, tightened more.

"Just rip the Band-Aid off," Danielle said morosely, picking up her coffee cup in two hands. "Married or gay, which is it?"

"You know he's not married."

"Gay. Damn."

"Well, here's the thing. He's not actually gay. More like...bisexual."

She perked up a little. "Oh."

"But he is involved with someone."

Her shoulders slumped again. "Oh."

"With me."

Danielle sat there blinking, then shook her head and said, "What?"

"He's involved with me. And with Chris. With both of us."

Danielle lowered her chin. "What are you saying, Kass?"

Kassidy rubbed her mouth, looked away, then looked back at Danielle. "Dag's living with us, because the three of us are in a relationship. We're polyamorous."

God. Other than Hailey, this was the first time she'd said it to someone outside of their triad. Her legs shifted under the table and her stomach churned.

"You are shitting me," Danielle whispered. "Seriously?"

"I'm not kidding." Kassidy met her friend's eyes so she'd know she was speaking the truth.

"Holy fucking fuck." Danielle stared at Kassidy with big eyes and parted lips, then said, "So what does that mean, exactly?"

Kassidy's eyes shifted one way, then the other. "It means... we're all sleeping together."

"So...you and Chris. Obviously. You and Dag...and..." she lifted an eyebrow, "...Dag and Chris?"

Kassidy bit her lip. "Yes."

She guessed she didn't have to tell her that much. She could've told her it was just Dag and her, and Chris and her. But she'd already told Danielle that Dag liked guys and girls, and...she just wanted it to be out there. She wanted her friend's honest reaction. Because if Danielle—her best friend who loved her—was going to freak out, what would the rest of the world do?

"That's hot," she breathed. "Holy shit. Chris and Dag... holy shit."

She grinned. "Oh yeah."

"I think I just had an orgasm," Danielle said. "A small one."

Kassidy laughed, some of the tension leaving her tight muscles. "Oh, Dani, I was so worried about telling you this. Not just because I knew you'd be disappointed about Dag, but because...I was afraid you'd hate me. Be disgusted with me."

Danielle's forehead creased. "I could never be disgusted with you. And, oh my God, Kass...I am so freakin' jealous!"

"Yeah well, put a lid on the jealousy because this isn't all that easy."

They started talking more, and their server got an earful when he arrived at the table just as Kassidy was saying Chris had never had anal sex before.

Danielle was awesome. All the tension leaked out of Kassidy, and she felt light and a little giddy. *Thank God. Thank God.* She reached a hand across the table and squeezed Danielle's. "Thank you, hon. I'm so relieved you're okay with this."

Danielle nodded, but tipped her head to the side. "I'm okay with it, honestly, Kass, and I get why you were worried, why you're not telling others. But I think people might accept it better than you think."

"Really?"

"Our friends anyway."

"You don't think some of the guys will be...homophobic?"

"Are you kidding me? You know those guys! Shit, Matt has had threesomes with Cole and Tyra."

Kassidy choked on her coffee. "What?"

"Oops." She put her fingers to her lips. "I wasn't supposed to say anything about that."

"Shit, Dani! I just told you something confidential! You have to keep this secret!"

She grimaced. "I'll try."

"Matt and Cole and Tyra?" Kassidy gave her head a shake. "Whoa."

"Yes. But there was no sword crossing."

Kassidy squinted, thought about that, then her eyes went wide as she got it.

Danielle cracked up. "You should see your face!"

Kassidy grinned.

"But see? It goes on all the time."

Kassidy slid her bottom lip through her teeth. "Um. Not so sure of that… Okay, maybe I am totally naive. The whole world is a big orgy and I've been missing out on it."

"You are kind of buttoned up, sweetie."

"Ack! Not you too!"

"What?"

"I'm not that girl! That good girl, all prim and proper."

Danielle grinned. "Well…"

"Dani!"

"Kidding. Sort of. This *is* kind of cool, you being the one involved in something so naughty."

"Yeah. Cool." Kassidy rolled her eyes.

"So nobody else knows about this?"

"Well, my sister does."

"Oh. Wow."

"She, uh, kinda walked in on us one day. And then…I went to see her when I was having that meltdown, and she talked me through it. She was actually pretty good about it. So I had to tell her how things worked out." Kassidy explained how she was trying to fix her relationship with Hailey.

"She's always been jealous of you," Danielle said, shaking her head. "I can't believe you couldn't see that."

Kassidy shoved her hair back from her forehead, leaving her hand there for a moment. "I can't believe it either. On the other hand, she didn't know I was jealous of her either. There's something about siblings…"

"True. My brother is a pain in my ass. Thank God for friends, right?"

"Right. You rock, Dani."

"I know."

They grinned at each other.

Chapter Eight

"Oh, that's the one."

Kassidy stood in front of Danielle in the dressing room at Nordstrom. It was Friday night and they were shopping for new dresses for Taisha's wedding, then meeting the girls for dinner and drinks. Danielle had found what she wanted early in the shopping trip, but Kassidy had been more difficult to please. She wanted something different, sexier, because she *felt* sexier, but trying things on she never would have picked out before resulted in a lot of rejections.

"It's really tight," she said, turning again in front of the mirror. "And low cut."

"It's not that low cut. You're only showing a little cleavage. It's sexy. And you have a great body. Show it off."

The dress was deep blue, heavy lace with tiny sleeves and a V neck, and was super fitted all the way down to where the scalloped hem ended just above the knees.

"How about the back though?" She turned. The dress had an even deeper V in the back that showed quite a bit of skin.

"See, that's the thing, you can show off your back and it's sexy, not slutty."

"Yes," Kassidy agreed. "I feel sexy in it. I feel like I'm so sexy I'm sleeping with two hot guys."

Danielle laughed. "Yeah. Work it, girl. With killer heels, that will be amazing. And speaking of two hot guys, which of them are you taking to the wedding?"

Kassidy went very still, staring at her reflection in the mirror. Then she tossed her hair back. "I don't know. I don't want to think about that."

Danielle shrugged. "Maybe you should talk to them about it."

"They know about the wedding." She frowned. Somehow, she'd pictured herself at the wedding with *both* her hot guys. "We'll figure it out."

"Oookay."

"You're right," Kassidy said. "This is the dress. Now the shoe department."

The dress was three hundred dollars—eep! But it was beautiful. She handed over her credit card and tried not to wince, imagining wearing it for Chris and Dag.

Half an hour later she sat in the shoe department with her narrowed-down choice of two shoes, one in each hand. "I love these," she said wistfully, holding up the nude-colored peep-toe pump embellished with crystals. "But they're so impractical." She lifted the other shoe, a simple pump with a high, spiky heel, also nude. "These I could at least wear to work."

Danielle nodded. "Go for the glam," she said. "Buy the impractical shoes for once. They're fabulous with that dress."

Kassidy bit her lip. "They are." She hitched her shoulders, squeezed her eyes shut briefly, then said, "Okay, I'll take these ones."

Loaded down with their dress and shoe purchases, she and

Danielle walked to the restaurant nearby where they were meeting Sarah and Tyra. After exclaiming over their purchases, they all ordered cocktails.

"It's fun to have a girl's night," Sarah said. "We haven't done this for a while."

Conversation flowed, drinks disappeared, dinner arrived. Tyra told them about her visit to the dentist where he'd diagnosed her with TMJ disorder. "I've been having headaches," she explained. "And then my jaw was hurting and I couldn't open it as wide. So now I'm getting some kind of appliance I have to wear at night. Apparently I grind my teeth in my sleep."

"Sexy," Danielle said, with a grin.

"Yeah, but the good thing is, I don't have to give blow jobs anymore."

The young busboy who'd stopped at the table to clear it froze. "Uh…I'll come back," he said, and vanished.

Kassidy stared at her friend. "That's a *good* thing?"

Tyra laughed. "What? You *like* giving blow jobs?"

"I do like it," Kassidy admitted, shocked that Tyra didn't.

"It's a good thing you do," Danielle said. "Seeing as you have two men."

Kassidy gave Danielle a bug-eyed look. Jesus!

"What?" Sarah asked slowly. "Two men?"

Oh Christ. Kassidy rubbed her forehead.

"Oh…ah…" Danielle covered her mouth. "Oops."

"Danielle!" Kassidy leaned forward. "I told you—"

"I know, I know, I'm sorry. Shit, my stupid big mouth—"

"What?" Tyra and Sarah both demanded at the same time. "What's going on?"

Kassidy closed her eyes and slumped back in her chair. "Shit."

"Kassidy has, uh, two boyfriends," Danielle said. "You guys

know Dag's living with her and Chris... Well...they're, like...together."

Stunned silence met this information.

"Are you shitting me?" Sarah breathed. Kassidy opened her eyes to see her openmouthed, wide-eyed expression.

"Shut the fuck up," Tyra said, wearing an identical look. "You and Dag? And Chris knows about this? And he's okay with it?"

Kassidy swallowed. "Yeah. He...participates." That was all she was going to say about that. She was not going to tell them that Chris and Dag were also lovers. She sent Danielle a pointed glance of warning.

"Whoa," Sarah said. "A threesome. But...every night?"

"Pretty much," Kassidy admitted.

Sarah blinked. "Holy shit."

"How long has this been going on?" Tyra asked. "Wait. I *so* need another drink." She lifted a hand to catch the attention of their server.

"Oh yeah, me too," Sarah said. "I think we all do. Another round here!"

"You can't be that shocked," Kassidy said to Tyra. "I heard you've had threesomes too."

Tyra now turned big eyes on Danielle. "Dani!"

"I'm in trouble tonight, aren't I?" she said in a small voice. "But, you guys, we shouldn't have secrets from each other."

"Some things are personal," Tyra snapped. Then she sighed. "Well. The truth is I guess I never wanted that known because I thought you'd judge us. But if you're doing it too..." she grimaced, "...guess not."

"I didn't intend to keep it a secret forever," Kassidy also admitted. "This is new. We're still figuring things out. I didn't want you guys to judge me either. But eventually...we want this to be a long-term thing, so I would have told you."

"Long term," Tyra repeated slowly. "So this isn't just a...thing."

Kassidy met her eyes. "No. I love Dag. And Chris."

"And, seriously, Chris is okay with this? That is hard to believe."

"I know it is," Kassidy said. "But he really is. The way he explained it is that he feels like he's giving me something when I'm with Dag. A gift. And he...he likes to watch."

"Fu-reaky," Sarah said. "I mean, in a good way. Nothing wrong with getting your freak on."

Sarah turned to Tyra. "You've had a threesome?"

"Yeah. More than once."

"Who with?"

Tyra pressed her lips together, then said, "Matt."

"Shut up! Oh my God!" Sarah fell back in her chair. "I am so jealous of you both."

Kassidy let out a long, slow breath. Holy hell. Like Danielle, Sarah was jealous of her. And Tyra wasn't judging her. She narrowed her eyes at Danielle. "I should be so pissed off at you."

Danielle gave her a winsome smile. "But you love me. Right?"

Kassidy sighed. "It was going to come out eventually. And I have no idea how I was going to tell you all. So I guess you sort of did me a favor."

"There," Danielle said. "You're welcome."

"So Kassidy's out with the girls," Dag said, lounging at one end of the couch with a beer in his hand. "What do you wanna do tonight?"

Chris glanced at Dag and caught the gleam in his eye. Oh fuck.

Which was exactly what Dag wanted to do, apparently, judging from the hot look in his eyes and the wicked lift of one eyebrow.

"I don't know," Chris said slowly. "Watch baseball?"

Dag rolled his eyes. "Shit, Chris. We're home alone..."

"Yep." Chris's dick thickened, even as his insides clenched. He gulped down some of his own beer.

"Chris." Dag's voice was soft. Chris looked at him. "What the fuck, man?"

"What?"

"You know what I'm saying. We've never fucked, just you and me. What's up with that?"

Put it right out there. Okay. "Nothing's up with that."

Dag narrowed his eyes at him. "Do you still feel like you'd be cheating on Kassidy?"

Chris's guts twisted. Here they went again, having another deep discussion about sex. But he considered the question. "No. I know you two have been together when I'm not around. And I know she won't feel that way."

"No. She won't. She offered to give us time alone. So what's the deal?"

He couldn't say. He couldn't explain it, even to himself.

"Look, buddy. I'm not gonna force you to do something you don't want to do. But I think you want to." Dag's eyes searched his face. "And I can be patient."

"Since when?" Chris smiled.

Dag rubbed the back of his head, looked away, then looked back. "I can." He lifted his chin. "You're the one who wants to be in control. You're in control. It's up to you."

Dag reached for the remote control for the TV and started channel surfing.

Chris sat there. He took another swallow of beer. He glanced at Dag, whose attention was on the television.

He didn't know what the deal was. It was true he didn't feel like he was cheating on Kassidy. He just liked it when she was there. And Dag was right—he did want it. Fuck, he wanted it bad. Since last weekend when Dag had talked about topping and bottoming and had basically told him he liked to be fucked up the ass, Chris had thought about it. A lot. He wanted that. His dick swelled and lengthened even more.

"Remember," Dag said quietly, not looking at him. "I love you."

Chris closed his eyes and lowered his chin. Yeah. And he loved Dag too, the bastard.

Then he got it. Got that he was hurting Dag. Dag wouldn't admit it, but Chris got it, thinking about how he'd feel if Dag didn't want to be with him. Kassidy was always telling him he needed to work on being more empathetic. Well, this was him trying, putting himself in Dag's place and realizing he was being a giant dickhead to the guy he loved.

"Shit," he muttered. "I'm an asshole."

Dag's lips twitched. "Huh."

Chris set his beer bottle on the coffee table, lifted his ass off the couch and planted it a few feet over, next to Dag. He removed Dag's beer from his hand, slapped it on the table too, and then grabbed Dag's face and turned it toward him. He dove into a hard, fast, fucking *hot* kiss.

"That's what I'm talkin' about," Dag muttered a long moment later.

Their eyes met and they exchanged evil grins, breathing hard. Then Chris kissed him again.

Fuck. Yeah. Fuck. Kissing Dag...his mouth hard, his tongue wet, rubbing against his tongue...yeah. He shifted closer, running his hand over Dag's chest, shoulder, neck, into his hair. He lifted his mouth off Dag's, tilted his head and went in again, deeper, hotter. Dag's hands grabbed him too, yanking him closer and they kissed, on and on, deep, sliding kisses, tongues licking, teeth nipping. A groan rumbled from Dag's chest and Chris felt it right to his groin.

Dag's hands roamed up and down his back and Chris shifted, leaning into him, pushing him deeper into the couch cushions. He sucked Dag's tongue, nipped his bottom lip, kissed across his stubbled jaw to his ear, then buried his face in Dag's neck when Dag's hand found his ass and gripped it.

They were making out, on the couch, all their clothes on, kissing and touching and it...was...hot.

Then Chris wanted skin and he shoved a hand up under Dag's T-shirt. He rubbed over Dag's pec, found the nipple and caught it in his fingers briefly. Dag's body twitched hard against his.

Heat rushed through Chris's body, excitement building, pounding in his veins. His dick ached.

"Yeah," Dag muttered. "Christ yeah. That feels good, Chris."

Hunger grew inside Chris, need blazed, and he shifted and slid to the floor between Dag's legs, fumbling with the belt, button and zipper of the shorts Dag wore. Dag spread his thighs wider, reclining on the couch, as Chris reached inside Dag's boxers and pulled out his straining cock.

"Fuck," Chris breathed, fisting it, rubbing his thumb over the slick head. He studied it with awe and fascination, stroking it. Veins pulsed and Dag let out a long, low groan.

"Suck me," Dag whispered hoarsely. "Want your mouth on me..."

Oh yeah. He wanted to do that. He licked his lips as he continued to study Dag, breathing in Dag's scent. He wanted to do it right. He wanted it to be good for Dag.

He opened his lips wide and directed the head of Dag's

dick, closing his eyes as he took him and swirled his tongue around the smooth head. Chris moaned his pleasure and Dag's hands came to Chris's shoulders, one curling around the back of his neck, not pressuring him, just holding him.

Dag's singular taste filled Chris's mouth—salty, male, musky. Fucking delicious.

Chris found a rhythm, sliding his lips up and down the shaft, absorbing Dag's taste. He slid his fingers beneath Dag's balls, fat and round at the base of his dick, bringing another long groan from Dag.

"Oh yeah," Dag whispered, his hips moving, picking up Chris's rhythm. "So fucking good…"

Chris licked and sucked until Dag grabbed his head and stopped him. "Okay," Dag gasped. "Enough…"

Chris looked up his body at Dag's face, enjoying the way Dag's chest heaved, the way his lips parted, the way his eyes glazed with desire. "Okay," Chris said with one last swipe of his tongue. Dag's dick quivered in response.

"Bedroom," Dag said. "We should go…in the bedroom."

"Okay," Chris agreed although he didn't feel the same need to move. Nobody was home…but, yeah, a bed was better. He rose to his feet, hand going to his aching cock. Then he grabbed Dag's hand and gave a hard yank, pulling him up and against him. He wrapped an arm around Dag's neck and gave him another fast kiss before turning toward the bedroom. They each started taking their clothes off on the way.

In the dim bedroom, Dag surprised him by shoving him toward the bathroom. "Shower," he said.

"What? Now? Jesus…" He was on fire and Dag wanted a shower?

"Humor me. It'll be quick. I wanna do dirty things to you…" he cranked on the water, "…and I want you clean."

Heat sizzled through Chris's veins at the idea of Dag doing dirty things to him.

Dag was right, it was quick, but fucking hot, Dag's soapy hands wrapping around Chris's dick, circling his balls, sliding up and down between his ass cheeks. Chris's body pulsed with need, his heart thumping against his ribs. He did the same for Dag, and then after a quick rinse, they stepped out.

Dag handed him a towel and they watched each other, Chris's mouth dry, his breathing labored. Dag stepped closer, slid a hand around the back of Chris's neck and pulled him in for another long, hard kiss, then released him.

"Bed," he said.

Chris had to grin. "I thought I was in control tonight."

Dag's lips twitched. "Oh yeah. Right."

"Whatever. Where were we…? Oh yeah, I was sucking your dick."

Dag groaned. "And doing a damn fine job of it." He threw himself down sideways on the bed, landing on his back. Chris looked at him, then rounded the bed.

"What're you doing?" Dag mumbled, head turning.

"Getting creative."

"Excellent."

Chris climbed onto the bed on his hands and knees over Dag's head then centered himself above him so Dag's cock was right in his face.

"Sixty-nine," Dag murmured, hands gripping Chris's bare ass. "Perfect." Then his fingers circled Chris's stiff prick. Pleasure shot through Chris as his muscles jumped.

Chris held himself up on one arm, grasping Dag's cock with his other hand and resuming his exploration, but, fuck, it was hard to focus when sensations were overloading him from behind, where he couldn't see, could only feel. He had to pause at one point, his head going back, eyes closed, Dag's pulsing shaft in his fist, as Dag's tongue slid up between his ass cheeks. "Jesus," he gasped, every nerve ending in his body catching fire.

Dag used his tongue and teeth and lips to torture Chris, sucking his balls into his mouth, teasing him and licking him. He even used his finger, slipping it into Chris's ass, bringing a sharp gasp from him, sensation shooting up Chris's spine. Chris gave a grunt of pleasure as Dag continued to tease there. Then Dag took Chris's shaft into his mouth, right to his throat. Chris's hips moved instinctively, fucking Dag's mouth, and a groan climbed Chris's throat again. Sucking in air, he bent his head again to take Dag into his mouth.

Holy fuck. Holy holy fuck. Sensation pounded through Chris, relentless, scorching hot, his balls so tight at the root of his cock as Dag tongued them again. Pressure built inside him and he slid his mouth off Dag's cock and gasped, "Gotta stop."

Now. He needed to fuck Dag now. Hot urgency boiled inside Chris as he moved off Dag and turned around. "Roll over," he told Dag.

Dag didn't move. "No."

Chris frowned.

"Face-to-face," Dag said, meeting his eyes, lifting his chin. "Fuck me face-to-face."

Chris stared at him. Heat whipped through his body once more. "Quit telling me what to do," he muttered. He slid off the bed at Dag's feet, Dag still lying sideways across the bed. Dag bent his knees and Chris grabbed his thighs and hauled him closer to the edge of the bed.

A wicked smile lifted Dag's lip. "It's called topping from the bottom. Get used to it. I do it a lot."

Truthfully, at this point Chris didn't mind Dag giving him direction because this was all new to him and he wanted it to be good for Dag. He looked down at Dag's groin. Lube. He needed lube. He took the two steps to the bedside table, yanked open the top drawer and grabbed the bottle. He gave it a shake and popped the top open as he moved back toward the side of the bed, Dag watching him with heated intensity.

Chris kneeled on the bed between Dag's thighs, spreading his own knees wide. He squeezed lube into one hand, lots of it, slicked it up and down his shaft. Fuck, that felt good, the slickness intensifying the sweet sensation. Then he dumped even more into his hand and, licking his lips, he reached for Dag's ass and spread the emollient there too, taking his time, watching Dag's face as he rubbed over his anus.

"Perfect," Dag breathed, pulling his knees back. "Oh yeah."

Chris capped the bottle and tossed it behind him. It hit the rug with a thud. Taking himself in hand again, he shifted his knees even wider, getting closer to Dag, then, emotion swelling in his chest, he fell over Dag's body and found his mouth.

They kissed, long and wet and intense, Chris's hips moving so his dick slid up and down over Dag's ass. They moaned in unison, Dag's hands gripping his back and holding him tight.

"Fuck me," Dag said.

"There you go again," Chris muttered, but they both gave choked little laughs as Chris pushed back up. He found his shaft, rubbed the slick head over Dag's anus, watching, so much sensation burning and twisting through his body, but also emotion building, knowing he was about to fuck the man he loved.

"I know you've done this before," Chris mumbled, glancing at Dag's face.

Dag closed his eyes briefly. But then he opened them and his gaze was steady and unblinking. Full of hope. Need. Aching vulnerability. And love. "Yeah," he said. "But never like this. With you. Love you, Chris."

"Yeah." Chris groaned. "Love you too." A hard shudder of

emotion worked down his spine. He pushed into Dag's body. Oh Jesus. Jesus Christ. He gritted his teeth at the pleasure that poured through him. His skin burned and tingled all over, his balls drawing up tight.

Opening his eyes, he looked down where they were joined now, intimately and perfectly, and pushed in deeper, the tight clasp of Dag's flesh on his, sublime. He studied Dag's cock, so big and thick against his belly, his balls full and round and smooth. Chris once more licked his lips, dazed and over-whelmed.

Dag's hands reached for him, clasped his thighs, his head lifting off the bed to also look down his body at where they were joined. His dark hair fell over his forehead, and noises climbed up his throat, soft, guttural noises of pleasure.

Fully seated inside him, aroused beyond measure by Dag's enjoyment and his own pleasure, Chris slid his hands up Dag's body, over his ridged abs, his flat pecs, then curved his fingers over Dag's shoulders and held on as he began to move.

Dag's eyes met his and they stared at each other with almost unbearable tenderness, moving together slowly. Then Chris lowered himself over Dag, sliding an arm beneath his head, and kissed him. They kissed deeply, tongues sliding and sucking, breathing hard, Chris's hips rocking into Dag's body, slowly and steadily.

Dag's hands moved to Chris's ass and gripped him, helping him move against him. Their mouths slid together again, then Chris lifted his mouth a breath away to look at Dag, both of them panting, soft noises escaping their throats, heat building. The love in Dag's eyes made Chris's throat clench and he gave another hoarse groan. "Fuck, man," he croaked. "Fucking amazing."

"Yeah. Love your cock in me. Perfect. Love it. Love you."

Chris kissed Dag's stubbled jaw, opened his mouth on him

and grazed his chin with his teeth, kissed and sucked the skin on the side of his neck. He buried his face there, breathing hard as his pace quickened. He kissed Dag's shoulder, his chest, found a nipple and sucked it into his mouth.

Dag's body twitched and he pulled in a sharp breath. He lifted his arms and folded them behind his head, watching Chris as he kissed and sucked. "Yeah, do that," he groaned.

Chris kissed his way back up, all the way to the underside of Dag's arm, tracing his tattoo with his tongue. He curled his hand around the back of Dag's head, kissed his ear, sucked on his earlobe. "Feels so fucking good," he muttered in Dag's ear, "fucking you."

"Close," Dag groaned. "So close…"

"'Kay." Chris pushed up again onto his hands, sucked Dag's other nipple briefly, kissed the middle of his chest, then straightened and gripped Dag's thighs. He was close too, dark pressure gathering, his skin buzzing. He watched Dag fist his own cock and start stroking, jerking in fast movements as Chris increased the pace and fucked Dag in a quick, hard rhythm. The mattress bounced beneath them.

Sensation built and twisted, hot and fierce. Cries fell from Dag's lips as his hand stilled on his shaft and Chris watched in awe as Dag's face contorted and he came in wrenching pulses, semen landing on his taut abs.

With a couple more slow, squeezing tugs on his dick, Dag groaned and then it slammed Chris too, hot and bright, electricity racing up and down his spine, the backs of his thighs tingling, sensation exploding inside him. He held himself tight at Dag's groin, eyes closing, cock jerking with each pulse of semen, draining him.

When his ejaculations had ended, he dragged open his eyes and looked at Dag. More emotion swelled in his chest, his heart still pounding, breathing still jagged. "Holy fuck," he grunted.

Their eyes met and something passed between them, something amazing and powerful and moving. "Love you. So much."

And once more he stretched out over Dag's sweat-dampened body to kiss him.

Chapter Nine

———————

KASSIDY OPENED THE DOOR OF THE CONDO LATER THAT NIGHT and pushed inside with her big shopping bags. "Hello! Anyone home?" She tripped into the living room, a wee bit buzzed from several cocktails with the girls. The television was on but silent. She took in the trail of clothes—men's shorts, T-shirt and boxers—and followed it to the bedroom, amused.

She paused in the open door and in the light from the living room saw Dag and Chris in bed, asleep, both on their bellies, faces toward each other, Dag's hand resting on the middle of Chris's bare back, the covers down around their waists. She smiled.

They were beautiful. Dag's dark, messy hair contrasted with the white pillow, the skin of his arm darker against Chris's golden tan. Her heart squeezed with love for them both.

She moved into the room, still carrying her purchases, and the noises caused Chris's eyes to flutter open. "Hey," he murmured, "you're home."

She sat on the bed next to him and leaned down to kiss his cheek. "I am. You guys are in bed early." He met her eyes and she smiled at him, wordlessly communicating with him. His answering smile melted her. She touched his face with her fingertips as Dag stirred next to him. "Okay?" she whispered.

He caught her hand and kissed her fingers. "Yeah. Great. I love you so much, Kass."

"Love you too." She looked at Dag, blinking his long, dark eyelashes, and she leaned across Chris to kiss him too. "And you."

"Babe. What time is it?"

"Just past ten."

"Huh. Guess we crashed."

"Yep." Her smile widened.

"How was your girls' night?" Chris asked, rolling over and shoving pillows behind him.

"It was…good. Except…" she sank her teeth into her bottom lip, "…Danielle sort of spilled the beans about us to Sarah and Tyra."

"Oh." Dag and Chris exchanged a look.

"You don't look too upset about it," Dag observed.

She sighed. "No. It was fine. Although…all we told them is that I'm sleeping with both of you."

"Ah. Okay." Another exchange of eye contact.

"Basically, they're jealous," Kassidy said with a grin.

"As they should be," Dag said.

Chris and Kassidy laughed.

"I bought a dress," she shared. "Wanna see it?"

"Sure." Dag too sat up and leaned back against the headboard.

"I'll put it on." She stood, eager to show them her sexy new dress. "I got shoes too, and they're so cute." She took her purchases into the bathroom and changed in there, smiling at her reflection in the mirror, excited to show off for her two guys.

Her two guys who'd apparently just had sex with each other. And looked so happy and content and satisfied. Too bad she'd missed it, but she was happy it had happened. She knew they'd needed it. This relationship was weird, for many reasons, but it struck her that not only was there one relationship between all three of them, there were also three relationships between each of them. And each of those relationships was unique and had to develop at its own speed and in its own way. The relationship between Chris and Dag was different than between her and Chris, or her and Dag, but no less important, and she wanted to make sure that they had the time and opportunity for it to grow as it should.

She turned and looked over her shoulder at the deep V at the back of the dress that made it impossible to wear a bra. She smiled with a little shiver, then slipped her feet into the pretty, impractical new shoes and walked into the bedroom.

Chris and Dag had flicked on the lamps on either side of the bed and were sitting up waiting for her. As their eyes turned to her and they both gave her an up-and-down look and a slow smile, she'd never felt more beautiful or more appreciated, or more loved.

She did a little catwalk pivot to show them the back of the dress.

"Nice," Chris said in a rough voice.

"Sexy," Dag agreed. "Wow, Kassidy, you're beautiful. Love that dress."

"And the shoes." She cocked a hip and extended one foot.

"Oh yeah. And the shoes. Hot."

"I love you guys." She beamed at them.

"We love you too, babe," Dag said. "Now take the dress off and get into bed here with us so we can show you how much."

. . .

Kassidy found herself actually tearful the next morning when Dag was packing a suitcase to leave. "I don't want you to go," she said, sitting on the side of the bed.

"I know. But I had to go back to San Francisco at some point. Now's a good time."

He'd decided that rather than go stay in a hotel or with her parents, he'd head back to California and spend the week taking care of the things he needed to do there.

"I know." She gave him a wan smile. "But I'm going to miss you. We both are."

"You'll be busy entertaining Chris's parents." But his eyes held a hint of shadow that told her he was going to miss them too.

"Ready to go?" Chris asked, entering the bedroom. "Luckily we only have to make one trip to the airport."

His parents arrived just after one o'clock and Dag's flight left at three, so Dag had suggested he'd go with Chris. He'd be early but he could kill time with his laptop.

"Pretty much," Dag said. "I didn't pack all my shit. That's okay, right? Your parents aren't going to come in here and start going through your closet, are they?"

Chris laughed. "Doubtful."

Kassidy's stomach hurt. "I hate this."

Dag kissed the top of her head. "I know, babe. But it's okay. We gotta do what we gotta do. I'll be back Friday."

He zipped up his case, and she trailed after him and Chris as they left the bedroom. She followed them to the door.

"Sure you don't want to come to the airport?" Chris asked her.

She shook her head. "I'll get the guest room ready. Need to vacuum and dust and clean the bathrooms before your parents get here."

"Okay." He kissed her forehead. "Back soon."

She turned to Dag, her bottom lip trembling. He wrapped his arms around her and she pressed up against him for a long, heartfelt kiss. She breathed in his scent, loving the feel of his arms around her. "Love you, babe," he whispered.

"I love you too." She sniffled but shaped her mouth into a smile. "Bye, honey."

Her throat hurt as she watched them walk out the door. She sucked in a long, shaky breath then squared her shoulders and headed for the cupboard with her cleaning supplies. She would distract herself from her sadness by scrubbing.

The guest room was all arranged and lovely, the main bathroom shiny clean with soft new guest towels laid out, the floors vacuumed and mopped, and a load of laundry had been done when Chris arrived home with his parents. Kassidy's stomach had tied itself into knots. She didn't know why. She'd met Chris's parents a couple of times and they'd seemed to like her, but this was the first time she'd seen them since moving in with Chris, and they were actually staying in their home.

They greeted her with hugs as Chris lugged their bags in.

"How was your flight?" Kassidy asked.

"It was fine, absolutely fine. On time and smooth. I'm such a nervous flyer, so that was good," Kathy Manness chatted.

"Chris will put your bags in the guest room," Kassidy said. "It's all ready for you."

"The condo is lovely," Mrs. Manness said, looking around. "And such a nice neighborhood."

"Yes. We like all the old trees."

"I'll show you around," Chris said.

"Would you like coffee, Mr. and Mrs. Manness? Or something cold to drink?"

"Call me Kathy," Chris's mom said with a smile. "And Hubbard." She nodded at Mr. Manness. "I'd love some coffee."

"That would be great," Hub agreed.

Kathy and Hub got a quick tour of the condo, then freshened up and unpacked a few things while Kassidy made coffee. Chris leaned against the counter, his mouth in a straight line. "You okay, hon?" she asked quietly, scooping grounds into the filter.

"Yeah..." he sighed and grimaced, "...I'm good."

They sat in the living room with his parents and chatted about their plans for the week. "I'm sorry Chris and I both have to work," Kassidy said.

"We'll find our way around," Hub said. "Kathy wants to go to Navy Pier. And some museums. And shopping." He rolled his eyes, but smiled.

"Hub wants to see a game at Wrigley Field," Kathy said. "He's already found out there's one Wednesday night. So maybe the boys can do that and Kassidy and I can do some girl things."

Kassidy smiled. "Sure. My parents would like to meet you this week too. They suggested maybe dinner together one night."

"Oh that would be lovely! I can't wait to meet them." Kathy beamed.

Okay. This was going all right. Like Dag said, they'd keep busy entertaining the family and the week would fly by.

Sure.

The favor of a reply is requested on or before July 21. _____ persons will attend.

Kassidy stared at the small RSVP card that had come with

Taisha's wedding invitation. The invitation that had come addressed to *Kassidy Langdon and Guest*. Guest—singular.

This probably wasn't covered in any of the wedding etiquette guides.

Her insides tightening, she sucked on her bottom lip. It was Thursday night and she was blessedly home alone for a little while, Chris having taken his parents to Navy Pier. They'd been busy every night this week, and although it had been nice getting to know Chris's parents better, there was always a tension there, knowing that they weren't being completely honest with his folks. She felt like she could never totally let her guard down or be herself around them, and it was exhausting.

She'd been poking through some papers, tidying up, and found the wedding invitation she'd been putting off dealing with. She'd pushed that whole problem out of her head, but now she had to do this.

She mentally sorted through her options. She could add a big *3* to the card and send it back. That was probably a bit forward. Maybe rude even. She could put *2* and take one of the guys. No. That was not an option. How could she do that? Leave Dag at home while she and Chris went to the wedding, or vice versa?

Was this what her entire life was going to be like? Making difficult choices? Denying the reality of their relationship? Always dealing with awkward situations like this? Because this wouldn't be the only one they'd ever have to deal with.

She picked up her cell phone and called Danielle.

"Hey," her friend answered.

"Where are you? Can you talk?"

"Yeah, I'm at home."

"Okay, good. Listen, I just went to RSVP to Taisha and I-I don't know what to do."

"Did you talk to Chris and Dag about it?"

"No. I just thought I'd figure it out myself. And Dag's been gone all week."

"Ah." Danielle let out a soft breath.

"I was all excited to go to the wedding, and I didn't want to deal with this. I guess I assumed both guys would go with me, which was stupid. Stupid! How can I do that? But I can't take just one guy."

"Huh. I dunno… Geez, Kass."

"Yeah." She sighed and poked at the card.

"Hey…I don't have a date for the wedding yet. How about you mark down two and I'll mark down two? We'll go together, and that way both your dudes will be there."

Something went soft in her chest. "I love you, Dani," she said softly. "That's so nice of you. But you don't have to do that."

"I don't mind. If I had a boyfriend, obviously it wouldn't work, but we can do it. Otherwise I don't know what to do. I suppose you could call Taisha and explain the situation to her and see if she'd be okay with you bringing one more person."

Kassidy's stomach cramped. That did not sound appealing to her. On the other hand…Dag going to the wedding as Danielle's guest didn't appeal to her either. Even if it *was* just for show. People would think Danielle and Dag were together. She imagined everyone asking about how they met, how long they'd been seeing each other… What would they say? It just made things even more complicated.

"Or I guess the other option is not going at all," she said.

Danielle made a noise of protest. "Oh no! You have to go. You already bought that dress and you're looking forward to it so much."

"I know. Seeing old friends…Taisha…" She sighed. "Well, I'll think about it."

"Let me know if you want me to take Dag. I mean, I

assume it would be Dag." Danielle hesitated. "You're not turning down the idea because I had that little crush on him, are you? Because I totally know he's yours, and this would just be to help out."

"No! That's not it. I know, Dani. I just...don't like the idea of him feeling...I don't know. Superfluous. Tagging along as your fake date...I don't want that for him."

"I understand. But if you change your mind, let me know. How're things going with the in-laws?"

They chatted a little longer. When Kassidy hung up, she looked at the card, then the phone in her hand. She swiped the screen to find her contacts, pretty sure she had Taisha's phone number in there.

Yes. There it was. What time was it in LA...? Earlier...okay. She tapped to call Taisha. She nibbled her bottom lip as she waited for her to answer.

"Hello?"

"Taisha! Hi! It's Kassidy Langdon."

"Kassidy! How are you, girl? *Where* are you?"

"At home, in Chicago. I'm calling about the wedding."

"Yay! Tell me you're coming, right? I can't wait to see you!"

"Well, I need to ask you a question." Kassidy's insides squeezed and she took a big breath. "I can bring a guest, right?"

"Of course! I saw on Facebook you and Chris moved in together."

"Yes, that's right." She swallowed. "But we have another person living with us..." Jesus, she didn't know how to say this. "The three of us live together."

"Oh. Um..."

"As in, he's my boyfriend too."

Silence.

Kassidy licked her lips. "So, I know it's a little out of the ordinary, but I wondered if it would be okay if I brought two guests."

More silence. "*Two* boyfriends?" Taisha said, disbelief clear in her voice.

"Yes," Kassidy whispered.

"Um. Wow. That *is* out of the ordinary." Taisha paused. "Uh...the thing is, we've already invited more guests than we originally planned, and somehow the guest list keeps growing, between Mark's parents and my parents, and...adding one more is really kind of—"

"I understand," Kassidy interrupted. "Totally. I shouldn't even have asked. I'm really sorry." She blinked at the sudden sting in the corners of her eyes. "I'll let you go."

"Okay. See you soon though! The wedding's not far away now."

"You bet."

Kassidy ended the call and set down her phone.

Once again she stared at the small white card with embossed script. She traced over it with a fingertip. Then she picked up a pen and wrote in a *0* for the number of persons attending, and slipped the card into the accompanying addressed and stamped envelope.

She swiped a tear.

Then she pasted on a smile as she heard Chris and his parents arrive home.

Dag's flight got in around four on Friday afternoon, so he'd told Chris and Kassidy not to bother picking him up. He was going to stay that night at a hotel, but he had to go to the condo first to get his car. So he might as well stay there for dinner and go to the hotel after. Kassidy was making dinner for Chris's parents for their last night in Chicago and insisted he be there.

He'd met Chris's parents a few times back in college but obviously hadn't seen them for a long time. He'd been gone from Chicago for six years. He'd liked them well enough when he'd met them, but he had to say that he wasn't looking forward to seeing them—in particular, Mr. Manness, after hearing how he'd fucked up his son.

Whatever. He'd smile and talk nice and then wave goodbye to them tomorrow and get back to fucking Chris up in a good way. He grinned.

He paid the taxi driver and hauled his luggage into the building, let himself into the condo with his key and shut the door behind him. Home.

Damn that felt good.

It wasn't just the place. It was the fact that Chris and Kassidy were there. Or would be soon, anyway, once they got home from work.

"Chris...?" A woman appeared. Whoa, Mrs. Manness. "Oh. Oh, it's Dag. Hello!"

"Hi, Mrs. Manness." Shit. For some reason he hadn't expected the parents to be there. "Nice to see you."

"I didn't realize you were coming this early."

"Uh, yeah." Again, shit. "My flight just got in. I left my car here 'cause Chris drove me to the airport last weekend. So I came here, rather than, uh, the hotel."

"Chris told us you've been staying with them since you came back to Chicago. I feel terrible that we displaced you from the guest room," she said. "Do you really need to go to a hotel tonight?"

He shrugged, still smiling, resisting the urge to head to the bedroom and change out of his jeans and into a pair of loose athletic shorts, then grab a beer and kick back on the couch. "No worries. It's not a problem."

He would have stayed in San Francisco one more day, but

because he'd booked last minute his choices of return flights were today or Monday, so he'd chosen to fly home today.

Chris's dad appeared behind his mom.

"Dag's here, Hub," she said.

Dag moved in to shake Mr. Manness's hand. "Good to see you, sir."

"You too, Dag, you too. Come on in."

Dag bristled. The guy was inviting him into his own home. Fuck this shit. He swallowed his annoyance and moved his suitcases to an out-of-the-way corner in the foyer.

"Can I get you a drink?" Mr. Manness said. "But you probably know your way around pretty well. How long have you been back in Chicago?"

"A couple of months."

"Looking for a place of your own?"

Dag gritted his teeth. "Oh yeah." He headed to the fridge. He was definitely having that beer.

"Chris tells us you're starting a new business," Mr. Manness said. "How's that going?"

He made conversation with them as they waited for Chris and Kassidy to arrive home, which was about forty minutes later. When they walked in, he jumped to his feet, unable to stop himself. Then he shoved his hands in his jeans pockets and tried to smile casually at them.

Kassidy walked into the living room first, dressed in one of her prim little business outfits—a tight, knee-length skirt in dark gray, a silky blouse in gray and pink, a pale-pink cardigan and a pair of high heels. Her shiny hair slid over her shoulders and she stopped dead when she saw him. He watched her suck in a breath and her eyes go shiny. Chris walked up behind her and set his hands on her hips. His eyes met Dag's.

The three of them stood looking at each other. It was a

wonder Mr. and Mrs. Manness couldn't feel the sparks snapping, the emotions swirling.

"Hey," Dag finally said, smiling. "How's it going?"

Chris's eyes heated in a sexy way that made Dag want to jump him. "Good. You?"

Kassidy smiled slowly, her own eyes making him promises of how she would greet him when she had the chance.

"Good." Banal. Innocuous. Just words, when what he really wanted was to grab them both, kiss them and hug them and tell them how fucking glad he was to be home.

Instead, he reached for his beer on the coffee table and took a couple of healthy swallows.

Kassidy bent her head for a moment, clearly trying to get her emotions under control. It took everything Dag had not to go to her and take her in his arms.

"So," Chris said, giving Kassidy a squeeze with his hands, then releasing her and walking into the living room. He loosened his tie with a sexy tug. "How was San Francisco?"

"Good. Got lots done this week."

"I'm gonna go change," Chris said.

"Me too," Kassidy said, and with one last longing look at Dag, they both disappeared into the bedroom.

Dag sat back down on the couch, trying to control the adrenaline rush that made him antsy, made his heart thud.

Chris emerged first, dressed like him in a pair of faded jeans, a *Dr. Who* T-shirt and bare feet. He too grabbed a beer from the fridge. "Mom, Dad...you want something to drink?"

"I'll make myself a rum and Coke," Mr. Manness said. "Kathy, you want some wine?"

"Yes, please."

Dag had had to stop himself from offering them a drink. Fuck.

When Chris returned, he took the chair adjacent to the

couch where Dag sat. "She okay?" Dag asked Chris in a low voice.

Knowing who and what he was talking about, Chris nodded, eyes warm. "Yeah."

Once again, Dag wanted to touch him but restrained the urge.

Kassidy came out wearing a pair of short-shorts and a loose camisole top. "Oh good, you all have drinks."

"What would you like, sweetheart?" Chris started to rise.

She motioned to him. "Sit, sit. I'll get it. I'm going to get dinner started."

"We should have gone out for dinner," Mrs. Manness said. "After a long week, you're probably tired."

"I'm fine." Kassidy smiled. "We've been out for dinner every night this week. I like cooking."

"She's a good cook," Dag offered. Kass smiled.

"What can I do to help?" Mrs. Manness asked.

"Nothing, nothing. I got some stuff ready last night."

Dag watched her, the way she spoke to Mrs. Manness so politely, the way she smiled, the graceful way she moved. Gorgeous. Sweet.

Fuck. He hadn't even been away a full week and he was all "absence makes the heart grow fonder" sappy.

He heard about the sights the Mannesses had taken in, the game Chris and his dad had gone to, Navy Pier, the boat cruise they'd taken, the trip to the top of the John Hancock Building and the deep-dish pizza they'd enjoyed. They'd taken Chris and Kassidy out for an outrageously expensive dinner at Bijoux to celebrate Chris's thirtieth birthday.

He and Chris got up to help set the table before Kassidy even asked, and he didn't give a shit what Chris's parents thought about his familiarity with where the place mats, dishes, glasses and flatware were stored. Fuck 'em. This was bullshit.

But it was necessary bullshit. And he'd survive.

They sat down to eat. Kassidy had prepared beef bour-guignon—delicious, tender pieces of beef in a rich wine sauce—served with fantastic little new potatoes.

"This is great, Kassidy," Mr. Manness said approvingly.

"Awesome," Dag agreed.

Kassidy met his eyes. "I know you like beef," she said.

Uh-huh. Did she make this for him? Damn. He liked that.

"What kind of wine did you use?" Mrs. Manness asked.

The dinner chitchat went on and on, and then Kassidy served dessert—cheesecake with fresh berries on top.

"I bought the cheesecake," she said apologetically as she served up pieces. "But it's from an awesome little bakery near here. And the berries are fresh local ones. I love the summer produce."

"It's great, sweetheart," Chris said. "But, God, I'm full."

When dessert was done, they lingered at the table with the last of the wine. Dag was feeling a helluva lot more relaxed, and he leaned back in his chair and turned the stem of his wineglass between his fingers. Yeah, he was gonna get through this.

"So, Mom and Dad," Chris said, "there's something we need to talk about before you go home tomorrow."

Chapter Ten

CHRIS'S GUTS HAD CHURNED ALL DAY AS HE'D TRIED TO DECIDE if he was going to do this. He'd changed his mind a dozen times. But walking in and seeing Dag there and not being able to greet him properly after being apart nearly a week had strengthened his resolve. He knew the chances were good that his parents weren't going to support him, but he couldn't live like this. They needed to know the truth.

It wasn't fair to Dag either. Chris wanted to acknowledge his feelings for him, not be ashamed of them. Dag deserved that. Everybody deserved that. Loving someone was never wrong, no matter who they were.

A few glasses of wine helped too. And when there was a lull in the conversation after dinner, he said the words.

"You need to know about my relationship with Dag and Kassidy," he began, not really sure what he was going to say, hoping he could find the right words. "Dag's been staying with us since he came back to Chicago because…" he looked at Dag, then back at his parents, "…he and I are in love."

The air in the room changed, became charged and electric.

He turned his gaze to his mom, who stared at him with wide eyes, then his dad, whose eyebrows had drawn down over narrowed eyes. Dad gave his head a shake. "What?"

"I'm in love with Dag. And with Kassidy. We're living in a polyamorous relationship. A committed relationship. They love each other too."

Mom touched her fingers to her throat as if clutching invisible pearls. "Chris…" Blinking rapidly, she glanced at Dad. "Hub…"

"Poly what?"

"Polyamorous. We all love each other."

Dad's face turned red. Then nearly purple. "Good Christ," he said. "What are you talking about? Have you lost your mind?"

Chris's mouth tightened. "No. I haven't. Look, I know this is hard to understand. Believe me, it took a lot for me to get it too."

"So you're telling us you're a faggot," Dad said.

Dag's chair hit the floor with a bang that made everyone at the table jump. He stood, strode around the table and grabbed Dad's shirt in a fist. "Watch what you say," he growled. "For one thing, he's your son. For another, he's the man I love."

"Get your filthy hands off me!" Dad shoved Dag away, pushing his own chair back. They stood and faced each other, glaring. Dag's hands curled into fists, but slowly lowered to his sides.

"Jesus," Dad said. "This is unbelievable. I can't even…" He shook his head. He looked at Kassidy. "And I thought you were such a nice girl. How can you…"

"I said, watch what you say." Dag stepped closer, the threat clear in his movements. Dad's hands came up. "Swear to God, if you insult her in any way, I will fuck you up. This is our home. You don't get to insult either of them. You listen. You may not understand. You may not agree. But you don't get to insult them."

Chris took in the set of Dag's jaw, the flash in his eyes, the color on his cheekbones. He was ready to blow. "Dag——" Chris began.

"I mean it," Dag snarled.

Dad's hands now curled into fists too, and Chris remembered the time his dad found him fooling around with his friend Cam. How he'd used those fists on him. Now, he and Dag stood off, waves of anger filling the room. Christ, were they actually going to get in a physical fight? Dad would be stupid to tangle with Dag, but if that happened Chris would have no hesitation about stepping in. He wasn't a kid anymore.

"I'm not listening to this," Dad snapped. "And I'm sure as hell not staying here with this…going on."

"I'm going to a hotel tonight," Dag snapped at him. "Relax."

"No you're not," Chris said. "You're staying here with us. This is your home."

"Chris——"

"Dag." Chris met his eyes and gave him an equally heated glare. "I'm serious. I want this out in the open."

Dad looked around the room, face still livid, mouth opening and closing. "I'm leaving."

Mom stood too. "Hub——"

"Going for a walk," he snapped. And he slammed out of the condo.

Mom slowly sat down again. Her face, in contrast to Dad's, had gone pale. She set trembling hands on the table and looked at Chris. "Chris. I don't understand this."

"I know, Mom."

Dag picked up the chair he'd knocked over and stood behind it, gripping the back.

"Are you…gay?" she whispered.

"Does it matter, Mom?"

She didn't answer that for a long moment, gazing at him with a cloudy expression. She looked down at the table, glanced at Kassidy, sent Dag an almost-fearful look, then swallowed. "I think it does matter," she said finally. "If you're not gay… maybe you just got mixed up in something you shouldn't have. You can't love two people. You and Kassidy—"

"I *can* love two people, Mom," Chris said quietly. "I do. There isn't a finite amount of love."

"But…he's a man." She again glanced at Dag.

"Yep, I am," Dag said shortly. "And I'm right here."

Mom's mouth tightened. "I think this is your fault, Dag."

Dag's jaw clenched again. "Okay, I'll take the blame, sure."

"There's no blame," Chris said. "It's nobody's fault, Mom. It just is."

"I can't…I just can't…"

"You maybe need some time to process this," Chris said. He looked at Kassidy, who hadn't said a word, sitting at the table, watching this with a wide-eyed look of stunned disbelief. "I understand that. You and Dad can go home and think about it. I wanted you to know the truth because, honestly, it really sucked to come home tonight and see Dag and not be honest about who he is to me, and to Kassidy."

"We were okay with you and Kassidy living together without being married," she said, "because we thought one day you would get married. But this…this is just wrong."

Chris closed his eyes at the wave of sadness that washed over him. "I'm sorry you feel that way, Mom. We know it's unusual, but we found each other and we care about each other. I don't think it's wrong to love someone. Or more than one someone."

"I-I don't… I'm going to go…to our room. Your father…"

"He'll come back," Chris said. "Probably better he cools down away from us."

Mom got up from the table and walked out, shaking her head.

Thick silence again filled the room. Then Dag snapped, "What the fuck, man?"

Chris looked at him, saw the anger still sparking in his eyes. "I had to tell them."

"Now? Jesus Christ!"

"Yeah, now! What the hell?"

Dag closed his eyes and shook his head. "Fuck me. I almost hit your dad."

"He deserved it."

Dag put a hand to his forehead, rubbing his eyebrows. "I am so fucking pissed right now...I gotta get out of here too."

Chris's jaw went slack as Dag, too, walked out of the condo.

His gaze went to Kassidy. She sat there, her hand flat on her chest, eyes wide, lips parted. She turned from watching Dag leave and their eyes met. "Oh my God," she whispered. "What just happened?"

"Shit," Chris muttered. He rubbed the back of his neck.

"He took his stuff," Kassidy said.

Chris blinked. "What?"

"Dag. He took his suitcase. It was by the door."

Chris frowned. "What are you saying?"

She swallowed, her bottom lip quivering. "He left."

"He'll come back."

Her eyes went shiny. "What if he doesn't? What are we doing, Chris?"

"What do you mean, sweetheart?"

She pressed her lips together and dropped her eyes. "This is causing so many problems."

"No. I mean, it is. But we knew that. It's worth it."

"Is it?" She lifted her eyes again, tears glimmering there. "Is it worth it? Your parents hate me now. They hate Dag. They're mad at you. They're your family."

"*You're* my family," he said roughly. "You and Dag."

Her lower lip pushed out and a tear slid down her cheek. "Oh, Chris."

"C'mere, baby." He pushed his chair back from the table and held his arms out. But Kassidy didn't come to him.

She stood, fingertips resting on the table. "I'm not sure anymore if we're doing the right thing."

"What?" He gaped at her, and then he was alone in the dining room as she, too, walked out.

For a moment he was numb. His head went empty. Then he felt a burning sensation, like a knife turning in his chest, and the burn spread out from there, through his whole body. His muscles went rigid and a fist squeezed at his throat. What the fuck had just happened?

Kassidy sat on the side of the bed. Everything inside her ached. She pressed her fingers to her burning eyes.

Great. Just effing great.

She didn't know what to think. She didn't know what to do. She just sat there hurting.

What if Dag didn't come back? What if he wasn't sure either if they were doing the right thing?

Was Chris really willing to continue with this if his parents hated both her and Dag?

Dag was pissed. Chris's parents were pissed. She was pissed at them too, truth be told. They'd known his parents weren't going to jump up and down with excitement over the fact that their son loved another man and was in a polyamorous relationship, but, even so, their reaction hurt.

She sucked in a breath and lowered her hands to the side of the bed. Drained of energy, her body heavy, she gave the covers a tug and slid beneath them, curled into a ball, still dressed in shorts and cami. Whatever.

She waited for Chris to come in.

But he didn't come.

She awoke in the morning with gritty eyes and stiff muscles. She stretched her legs out and turned her head. Chris slept beside her. He must have come to bed after she fell asleep.

Dag wasn't there.

Had Hub come back after his walk? Had he talked to Chris?

She bit her lip, then slid out of bed to use the bathroom.

God, she hadn't washed her face before she'd fallen asleep and mascara was smudged beneath her eyes. Her puffy eyes. She grimaced at her reflection as she brushed her teeth, then stripped off her wrinkled clothes and stepped into the shower.

Chris slept on when she emerged.

She dressed in yoga pants and a tank top and quietly left the bedroom. The condo was quiet, the door to the guest room closed. She passed on the TASSIMO and started a big pot of coffee, then sighed as she took in the mess in the kitchen. Shit. After the big scene last night, nobody had bothered to clean up.

Luckily she'd put away leftovers between dinner and dessert, and some of the dishes had been loaded into the dishwasher, but dessert plates, forks and wineglasses still sat on the dining room table.

She cleared the table, noted the number of empty beer bottles sitting on the counter. Looked like Chris had had a few by himself. Unless he and his dad had sat down and had a heart-to-heart over beers.

Not likely.

By the time the coffee was ready she had the kitchen

cleaned up. She poured herself a cup and wandered into the living room to look out the window. Rain drizzled down from a pale-gray sky, weighing down the branches of the maple trees, dripping from the leaves, running down the big window. She leaned her forehead against the cool glass.

Kathy and Hubbard's flight left at noon. It was nearly eight thirty. Should she wake them and Chris? They'd need to leave for the airport soon. Ugh. First, she'd deal with Chris.

Back in the bedroom, she set down her coffee and sat on the bed, leaning toward Chris. She gave his shoulder a nudge. "Chris? Honey?"

He stirred and rolled toward her. "Wha…?"

"Do you need to take your parents to the airport? It's eight thirty."

He blinked at her, eyes unfocused. Then he sighed. "No. They left last night."

"Oh."

He rubbed his face. "They went to stay at a hotel. Took a taxi."

"Oh," she said again. "Okay. Were they still…upset?"

"Hell yeah."

She bit her lip. "I'm sorry, Chris."

"Fuck, you don't need to be sorry. They're the ones who are being dicks."

"Chris."

"Whatever. I'm done. I tried to talk more to my dad when he came back. It's like talking to a wall. He'll never change. But that's his problem."

She closed her eyes, sadness filtering through her. "I guess that's true." She paused. "D'you want to go back to sleep?"

"Nah. I'm awake now. That coffee smells good."

"I'll go pour you a cup." She moved off the bed and retrieved her own mug.

Chris followed her out, naked except for his blue- and white-striped boxers. "That was ugly last night," he said, taking the mug from her when she'd added the cream and sugar he liked. "Sorry you had to go through that, Kass."

"Yeah." She hesitated. "I wish you had told us you were going to do that."

He stared at her. "Oh."

"I mean, I'm glad you did it. But...we should've talked about it first."

"Shit." He slumped against the counter. "D'you think that's why Dag took off?"

"I don't know. Maybe that was part of it. He was pissed at your dad, for sure, but, damn, Chris, that was a big decision to make without even telling us. You have to *talk* to us."

He blew out a long breath and rubbed his forehead. "Yeah. You're right. Jesus. I'm sorry, Kass."

"But you don't need to apologize for your parents' behavior."

"I know, but I feel bad. You didn't deserve that. You haven't done anything wrong, Kass. You know that, right?"

There'd been a time when she'd felt that way, when she'd felt like things had gotten so messed up, people had gotten hurt because of her desire to be a little bit bad and have a naughty threesome. Dag had told her that what they'd done didn't make her a bad person, because she'd never intended to hurt people, and what she'd done had been out of love.

She gave him a crooked smile. "Oh, Chris. This is a mess."

"We knew it was going to be messy. But we all agreed to do it anyway. Because it's worth it." He moved closer and set down his coffee to pull her into his arms. "I love you, Kass. That makes anything worth it."

"I love you too. But it's hard."

"I know." He leaned his forehead against hers. "I know. But we can do it."

"What about Dag? I feel sick that he left."

"I came back."

Kassidy's and Chris's heads both whipped around at Dag's voice from the kitchen door. He stood there, gripping each side of the doorframe in his hands, dressed the same as Chris, in a pair of boxer shorts, his dark hair messed up, his jaw shadowed with stubble. So beautiful.

"Dag," she breathed.

"What the hell, man?" Chris muttered. "When did you get home?"

Dag hitched one shoulder. "I don't know. Around two in the morning. You two were asleep. The guest room was empty, so I crashed there." He lifted an eyebrow. "Your folks didn't stay last night?"

Chris shook his head. "Went to a hotel."

Dag lifted his chin.

Tension crawled up Kassidy's spine, tightening her muscles. The air in the room vibrated.

"Why did you leave?" she asked Dag quietly.

"I was pissed off."

"Got that, man," Chris muttered.

"Yeah. I was pissed at you." Dag scrubbed a hand over his face. "I just wished you had told me you were gonna do that. I wasn't ready. I lost my mind. I nearly punched your dad. That was not cool."

"Okay, yeah. I should have talked to you guys first. I get it. But I thought about it all week, and I didn't know for sure I was going to do it until that moment."

Dag nodded and met Chris's eyes. "That took guts."

Kassidy's heart swelled. She looked up at Chris. "That's true, honey," she whispered. "A lot of guts."

"Yeah, well, it took guts to stand up to my dad for insulting me and Kass." Chris swallowed. "Meant a lot to me that you did that."

"Fuck. Meant a lot to me that you told them," Dag said.

And then the three of them were together, one of Dag's arms around Chris, the other around Kassidy, and she was crying, but smiling.

"I love you guys…" she sobbed, "…so much."

"Kass, what you said… about not being sure about this anymore…"

"I'm sorry. I'm sorry I started to have doubts."

"There are gonna be more hard times," Chris said. "We gotta get through them together."

"Yesterday…" she sniffled, "…the wedding invitation… I felt so bad. And then we came home, and, Dag, you were here, and I couldn't even hug you, and I missed you so much last week…and then your parents being so shitty to us… Sorry…"

Chris huffed out a laugh and kissed her hair.

"What about the wedding?" Dag asked, brushing Kassidy's tears away with his thumb.

"The invitation was to me. And one guest."

"Oh. Of course. Fuck."

"So I called Taisha to see if I could bring two guests."

"You did what?" Dag and Chris both said at the same time.

"I didn't know what else to do. I couldn't take just one of you and leave the other at home. Danielle offered to take Dag as her guest, but that didn't feel right. I wanted you there with me. Both of you. So I called Taisha and asked her, and she was kind of… Well, I don't blame her—you can't just ask to add another guest to the list. But it made me feel sad, and so I sent the reply back saying we're not going."

"Hell," Dag said.

"Shit," Chris said.

"That took guts too, Kass," Dag whispered. "Love you."

"Yep," Chris said. "Brave girl. I love you too."

She smiled through her tears at that.

"And you bought that sexy new dress," Dag commented.

Her smile went crooked. "I can take it back."

"Hell no. You look fucking awesome in that dress."

They each kissed her cheek. "We'll take you out somewhere special," Chris said. "You can wear the dress."

She closed her eyes, emotion expanding so big inside her she squeezed her eyes tighter as more tears gathered.

"You should have told us about the wedding invitation, babe," Dag said. "We're here for you. Always."

"You weren't here. You were in California."

"I'm always here," he repeated firmly. "Even if I'm not. You pick up the phone and call me, or whatever. That goes for both of you. And, anyway, I'm not leaving again." He grinned. "Man, I need a Coke."

Epilogue

"HAPPY BIRTHDAY, DAG." KASSIDY KISSED HIS CHEEK.

He stood inside the condo, looking around at the crowd of people. Wow.

He'd known Kassidy was planning a party for him, like Chris's a few weeks ago, so it wasn't a surprise, but he hadn't realized she'd invited her whole family, as well as their friends. Hailey was there, and her parents sat on the couch side by side, Dave's arm stretched along the back behind Hope.

Their reaction to Kassidy telling them about the three of them had been markedly different than Chris's parents'. They'd been upset, yeah, but they'd listened to the three of them and tried to understand. Dave had been shocked at first. Hope, not so much. Kassidy had been right, her mom was pretty perceptive and had picked up on Dag's feelings for Kassidy already.

Hope had explained her concerns though, concerns because she knew there were going to be some tough moments in life if they wanted that kind of relationship. It wasn't that she thought they couldn't deal with those problems—it was just that, as a mother, she didn't want her daughter to *have* to deal with them. Dag got that. Every parent wants their kid to have a perfect, happy life. But life's not like that—for anybody. So they'd have a few extra challenges. They knew that.

"Thanks, babe," he murmured, sliding an arm around Kassidy's waist to give her a squeeze. Then Chris came up to them both and laid a hand on his shoulder. Their eyes met and they shared a smile.

"The big three-oh," Chris said. "Old man now."

Dag grinned.

He noticed the bar set up in the dining room. "You hired the same bartender."

"Yeah," Kassidy said. "He was fun."

Dag started to ask who was paying for it, then kept his mouth shut. If they wanted to do this, fine. They knew what they could afford and what they couldn't, and he'd find other ways to spoil them.

"I could use a beer," he said, moving into the room. He shook hands, hugged, slapped shoulders with their guests, until he got to the bar and requested his drink. The bartender slid him a cold one with a smile.

He'd had a late business-dinner meeting that he'd had to schedule on his birthday, but he'd promised Chris and Kassidy he'd be there as soon as he could. His business was moving forward. He had investment money, he had the prototype designed and tested, and he'd hired a marketing guy who'd already lined up potential clients, one of whom they'd met with tonight. And looked like they would be their first sale.

That was just one more reason to celebrate.

He opened gifts, laughed with everyone, enjoyed the evening. By the time all the guests had finally left at nearly three in the morning, everyone having so much fun they didn't want to leave, he realized he hadn't gotten a gift from Chris and Kassidy.

Not that he was all about the gifts. Having them in his life was gift enough.

What a fucking sap he'd turned into. He grinned.

He helped clean a few things up before they headed to bed. In their bedroom, he unbuttoned his shirt and tugged it out of his dress pants, then pulled it off his arms and dropped it on the floor. He paused, then with a wry smile he picked it up and tossed it in the hamper, like Kassidy kept on him about. He yawned and used the bathroom. When he emerged into the bedroom, lit by only one lamp beside the bed, Chris and Kassidy were sitting on the bed. Chris sat on the side, Kassidy in his lap, one arm around Chris's neck. She held a small wrapped package.

Dag grinned. "I thought maybe you forgot to buy me a present."

"Well," she said. "We had a hard time. Because what do you buy a thirty-year-old multimillionaire? A Ferrari? A swimming pool?"

He laughed.

She patted the bed beside them and he sat, bare-chested, and accepted the package.

As soon as he got the wrapping paper off, his chest clenched. He stared at the glossy black box, then slowly pulled the lid off. Inside was a silver pendant.

He lifted his eyes to meet first Kassidy's, then Chris's.

"Thank you," he said hoarsely. He pulled it out.

It was the same charm he'd given Chris for his birthday— Trilogy—this one on a black cord.

"You know what it means," Chris said in a low voice.

"Yeah." He swallowed. "Kass, can you help me…?"

He turned his back and she fastened it at the nape of his neck. The charm felt cool but quickly warmed to his skin.

"That's not all we got you," Kassidy said. "We *are* getting you a swimming pool."

His forehead tightened. "What?"

She glanced at Chris. "We talked about it and we do want to move. We want to pick out a place with you. It'll be ours. And we'll even let you spend some money on it. But it has to have a pool."

Emotion swelled inside him. "Awesome. Thank you." He touched the charm resting on his sternum.

Chris cleared his throat. "Kass, can you move?"

She shifted and Dag reached for her, pulling her onto his lap. He kissed her mouth, slow and sweet, and murmured another "thank you" as Chris moved to the dresser across the room.

"I know it's not your birthday," Chris said, turning, obviously speaking to Kassidy. "But I got you a present too."

Kassidy blinked, then smiled. "Okay. I like presents."

And Chris handed her another box, this one not wrapped and instantly recognizable as being from the same little jewelry shop. She sucked in a breath and opened it to reveal a third pendant—same charm—this one on a polished silver chain, glittering in the lamp light.

Her head snapped up to look at Chris, and Dag hugged her tighter. "Oh my God," she whispered. "Thank you. Of course we should all have one."

Chris moved behind her to fasten the chain around her neck.

"Beautiful," he said. He kissed Dag, then her. Then he dropped to a crouch in front of them. "I want you both to have rings," he continued. "As well as the pendants. Some day."

Dag went very still and felt Kassidy do the same in his arms.

"I know these are a symbol of our love," Chris said. "But I

want to have the traditional symbol too. It won't be completely traditional. But I want people to look at your left hands and know you're taken."

"And you too," Kassidy whispered, grabbing his left hand.

"Yeah. Me too. I want to wear your ring. I don't know what we're going to call this relationship. Can we call it a marriage? A commitment? What do we call each other? Husband? Wife? Partner?"

"We don't need to label it," Kassidy said. "It's ours. Labels and social norms and traditions aren't enough to describe our relationship. It's not as simple as a word. It's...love."

Dag squeezed his eyes closed, his throat clogging. Yeah.

Some people might be depressed over turning thirty. Not him. How could he be depressed when he had so much in his life, more than he ever thought he would? And not only did he have Chris and Kassidy, he had her family—her parents, her fractious sister, who nonetheless had accepted him into their family, and that meant a lot to him. Accepted him as who he was, flaws and all.

And friends. Yeah, some of those people were ones he'd gone to college with, but he hadn't been one to make the effort to stay in touch when he'd moved away. He'd wanted to leave his life in Chicago behind, but now he saw what he'd lost by doing that.

Thank fuck he'd come back. Thank fuck he'd taken that chance. It hadn't even remotely turned out like he'd ever dreamed. It had turned out better.

He'd grown up without a lot of love, spent most of his life trying to pretend he didn't care, and now he had two people who loved him, who'd managed to convince him he was someone worth loving. But being loved wasn't the only important thing—having someone to love was huge too. Because if you couldn't give love, how could you receive it?

And now he'd learned that the more love you give, the more love you *have* to give…and the more you get in return.

"This is the one."

One month later, Kassidy turned in a circle in the middle of the living room, surveying the beautiful architectural details —the crown molding, the deep baseboards, the shiny hardwood floors. The white fireplace was flanked by white built-in bookcases. Sun shone through two large mullioned windows.

"It's definitely big," Dag said.

"There's no pool though," Chris added.

"True," Dag agreed. "But the yard is big enough for one. We can put one in."

"I love it," Kassidy said softly, hands clasped in front of her. "Do you guys?"

"Yeah." They both spoke.

"Can we really afford it?"

"Yeah," Dag said roughly. "We talked about this."

Warmth expanded in her chest. "Yeah. I know."

They'd started looking at condos, nice modern lofts in high-rises, then somehow ended up looking at houses. Kassidy had tentatively broached the subject of kids during the house hunt, and even though none of them was ready for that step yet, they all agreed it made sense to move into a family home where they could stay long term.

Between the three of them, it hadn't been easy to find something they all loved. The guys all had specific things they wanted. Chris wanted to make sure the foundation was strong, the electrical and plumbing were updated. Dag wanted a pool. Kassidy wanted lots of bedrooms and bathrooms, and a big kitchen. They'd found one that had all those things, but the kitchen was old and out of date, and although she'd been willing to remodel the kitchen and that actually would have been fun, the price of the house, along with the cost of a kitchen remodel and the time involved in that, made all of them think twice.

But this one…had it all. Almost all. But like Dag had said, they could put in a pool. The price was good enough that it would be economically feasible, and other than the pool, it was in move-in condition.

With big main-floor rooms, Kassidy could imagine a few kids running through them, playing, then heading out to the parklike backyard. She hadn't mentioned it to the guys, but she'd made sure the schools nearby were good. She could see herself in this big kitchen with kids sitting at the island.

Not right away. But someday.

In the meantime, they'd all have room to spread out. They'd discovered they all needed their own space and alone time once in a while, and the condo they were in wasn't that big.

"Okay," Dag said. He turned to Brian, the realtor they'd been tormenting. "Looks like this is the one."

Brian grinned. "Thank God. I was starting to think you were never going to agree on something."

He hadn't blinked over the fact that three of them were buying the place. What did he care, as long as he got his commission? But he'd been great, patient and understanding of their needs.

"All right, boys," Kassidy said with a smile, "we're buying a house."

The pool party ten months later was to celebrate the installation of the new pool and Chris's and Dag's thirty-first birthdays in a combined party. Friends and family were there, just like a year earlier, only this time Jeff and Sarah had a baby, little Jaden.

"How's business?" Chris asked Hailey.

"Excellent." She lounged back in a chair, wearing a tiny black bikini, sipping one of the watermelon-basil mojitos she'd whipped up in the kitchen. "I signed two new clients just this week." She'd gone ahead with her idea of starting her own mixology consulting company. Surprisingly, she'd come to Dag, Chris and Kassidy for business advice on all kinds of things—accounting, finances, marketing and training. They'd all been happy to contribute their individual areas of expertise and help Hailey get started, and it seemed things were going well.

Kassidy appeared, also wearing a tiny bikini, hers pink and semicovered with a sheer white tunic that ended just above her knees. Her skin was tanned from all the time in their yard, as she'd discovered a passion for gardening. Her brown hair hung loose to her shoulders, shiny in the sun, and she held a pink-wrapped bundle in her arms. Jaden.

Chris smiled at her, so beautiful, gazing down at the baby girl in her arms.

"Isn't she gorgeous?" Kassidy crooned, touching a finger to one cheek.

"*You're* gorgeous," Chris said.

Kassidy met his eyes and they exchanged a smile. "Want to hold her?"

"Uh…no."

"Oh come on. There's nothing to be afraid of."

"I don't know anything about babies."

"You better learn."

He narrowed his eyes at her. Holy fuck. She wasn't about to tell him she was pregnant, was she?

Then she laughed. "Don't look so terrified! I'm not pregnant. But if you want to be a father, you better be okay with holding a baby. Both of you," she added as Dag approached.

Dag too was tanned, even darker than Kass, due to his deeper skin tone and dark hair. His blue board shorts sat low on his hips and Chris took a moment to admire him too.

"I don't mind babies," Dag said, moving closer. "But I actually prefer it when they start walking and talking. Kids are fun. But she *is* pretty cute."

"You guys'll make good dads," Hailey said.

"Thanks." Chris gave her a crooked grin. "My parents don't share that opinion. They think it will be cruel to bring a child into our 'arrangement', as they call it."

Kassidy's mouth tightened at the mention of Chris's parents and their opinions about the three of them. She and Dag were still pissed at them, although the anger had faded. Chris himself had just moved on. He had what he wanted in life…people who loved him. If his parents didn't want that for him and couldn't deal with it, it was their loss.

His eyes caught the flash of the enormous diamond on Kassidy's left hand. His and Dag's diamond. They'd picked it out for her together and they'd blown her away with it, a unique design with a round solitaire set in a wide swirl of platinum…not an engagement ring, but not just a simple wedding band either. Then the three of them had gone shopping for rings for him and Dag, settling on the same for both of them, also platinum, smooth bands with beveled edges.

The rings were a traditional symbol of their untraditional relationship.

Their lives weren't perfect. There were still people who couldn't accept their relationship, although surprisingly few, and there were still people who didn't know about their relationship. They'd become friends with a few others in poly relationships whom they'd met through a counselor who'd helped them work through some of the issues they faced. They had worries and problems. Kassidy's dad had had a heart attack a few months ago, but was okay now. They all had problems at work. Jeff and Sarah now had a beautiful baby, but she'd had complications during her pregnancy and ended up in the hospital the last month before Jaden was born, scaring them all. Kassidy had freaked out about Dag wanting to go skydiving, and Chris and Dag rolled their eyes when Kassidy bugged them about putting the empty peanut butter container back in the cupboard and leaving their wet towels on the bathroom floor.

They argued about stuff like Chris working late too many nights when Kassidy wanted to get home, and, yes, they argued about money, not that they lacked it, but there was still a bit of a power struggle between him and Dag over who paid for what. They argued about leaving the toilet seat up and who should vacuum, because they all fucking hated vacuuming, what movies to watch, and the fact that Dag had to eat beef at damn-near every meal.

But everyone argued about crap like that.

Then they made up. They loved each other. They wanted this to work because the alternative was too agonizing to even consider.

That night after everyone had gone home, they turned out the lights, climbed the beautiful oak stairs up to their master suite and got into bed, talking about the party, sharing bits and pieces of it with each other, touching and kissing, legs twined together.

And the three of them moved together, finding their unique rhythm...their rhythm of three.

Author Note

Thank you so much for reading the Rule of Three complete collection! Make sure you're on my mailing list for news about my next releases. If you enjoyed Reward of Three please consider leaving a review at the retailer of your choice or at Goodreads to help other readers find my books. You can also contact me at info@kellyjamieson.com to tell me what you thought of it or ask me any questions!

And enjoy this sneak peek at another of my ménage stories...

Excerpt ~ Reward of Three

BY KELLY JAMIESON

She didn't know how to tell them.

There was the straight-up, open and honest way. There was the sneaky cute way. There was the vague hinting way.

Kassidy wasn't sure if she was any good at sneaky and cute. Maybe if she thought about it enough, she'd come up with an idea. Vague hints might work. But sometimes her guys were clueless. They also weren't always good at subtle. That left straightforward.

But this was a pretty momentous moment. Heh.

In the end, the sneaky cute way came to her like a divine intervention at the most mundane time. Friday nights they often stayed home and watched movies or played board games. Dag had scoffed at the tameness of it all, but as the three of them had settled into their poly relationship, he'd been the first to stretch out on the couch with a beer Friday night and ask what movie they were watching or what game they were playing.

"Scrabble," Chris said tonight.

There was a brief argument between the guys because Dag

hated Scrabble. Kassidy sipped her herbal tea and watched them with a smile. Then the Scrabble board came out.

"Man, we're acting more and more like old people," Dag commented, lining up his tiles. "Friday night sitting at home playing Scrabble."

Chris laughed, eyes on his own tiles. "You *are* old. Besides, we're going out tomorrow night."

Kassidy nibbled her bottom lip, her insides fluttering. Was this going to be good news for them? For Dag? If he was worried about staying home on a Friday night, living a staid, boring life…well, this might not be news he wanted to hear.

But they'd talked about it. They'd all agreed. They wanted this.

The game began, and Kassidy glumly surveyed her tiles. She had nothing. She managed to add a couple of tiles to Chris's "ascot" and create "cat". She rolled her eyes. The game continued and then Chris spelled the word "gnat". Kassidy looked at her tiles and the letters P, R and E jumped out at her. Pregnat. Her eyes widened. And then she saw the I and M tiles. Her heart started thumping as she waited for Dag to take a turn, praying he wouldn't touch that word.

He didn't.

Her fingers trembled as she tried to place the little tiles on the board, messing them up, then straightening them. When she drew back, she read her creation: IMPREGNAT.

She looked up at Chris and then Dag. They both frowned at her word.

"That's not a word, sweetheart," Chris said. "You need an E on the end."

"No," she said, "actually I need another N. Right here." She touched the tiles with her index finger. Then she totally cheated by picking up an N from another word and moving it there.

"You can't do that," Dag objected.

She laughed. She'd been so right about the subtle thing. "Oh my God. Read it."

They both looked at the word again and then she saw their faces change at the exact same moment as understanding dawned. They turned shocked eyes to her and she smiled at them. They blinked and in unison, their gazes dropped to her stomach, then back up. She nodded.

"Fuck," Dag breathed. In a flash, they were both kneeling in front of her where she sat on the couch.

"Sweetheart. Really?" Chris gazed at her. "You're pregnant?"

"Yes."

"Fuck," Dag said again.

"Holy shit," Chris said.

They both reached for her and she slid an arm around both their shoulders, bending her head toward theirs. The corners of her eyes stung and she squeezed them shut.

"You okay, babe?" Dag asked in a rough voice that sounded like he was near tears. "Feeling okay, I mean?"

"I feel great."

"When is this gonna happen?"

"According to the website I used, we're due November 9. I haven't been to the doctor yet, but I did two pregnancy tests to make sure."

"You need to go to the doctor!" Chris said.

"I will. I have an appointment next week." She smoothed a hand over his dark gold hair. "I'm fine."

"Wow. November. Okay." Chris swallowed. "Wow."

She tightened her arms around them and they hugged, heads together. "I know. It is pretty wow."

Emotion rose inside her and she felt it in her guys too, their short breathing and vibrating bodies.

"This fucking scares the shit out of me," Dag muttered.

She touched his dark hair. "Why?"

He lifted his head and looked at her, lips pressed together. "It's just...a lot."

She studied him. "Talk to us." She suspected where his thoughts were going. "Wait, get off the floor, both of you."

They rose and sat beside her on the couch, flanking her as they almost always did, on the couch or in bed, or walking down the street. They were always there for each other, but even more, they were always there for her, protecting her, caring for her.

"Why are you scared?" she asked again.

Dag took in a breath. "I never had a dad growing up. My dad didn't give a shit. He took off when I was three. I never had any kind of father figure." He met Kassidy's eyes. "I don't know how to be a dad."

"Yes, you do." She laid a hand on his darkly stubbled cheek. "All you have to do is love our son or daughter. And besides, I don't know how to be a mom."

"At least you had a mom who gave you some kind of good example. Even my mother was a crappy parent. What if I screw up? What if I turn out to be like them?"

"You won't." Chris spoke up. "You're not like them. And Kass is right. None of us knows how to do this. We'll figure it out together. We'll be there for each other like we always are."

They didn't mention the things they'd talked about in the past when they'd considered the decision to have children. They didn't talk about bringing a child into their unconventional relationship. They didn't talk about the kinds of reactions their child might encounter when people learned about their unusual family. They didn't talk about who was the biological father of the baby...because they'd all agreed it didn't matter.

They were all three going to be parents to this baby and genetics didn't change that.

They'd learned a lot from the people they'd met through the counselor they'd seen when starting this relationship. They'd become friends with other poly couples, including some with children. They were fully aware that there were going to be obstacles and hard times. But they were also confident that they could give a child—or two, if Kassidy got her way—enough love and support that their children would be strong and resilient and able to deal with whatever life brought them.

They'd shared their doubts and misgivings, but the desire to have a child and be a family had prevailed and they'd stopped using any kind of birth control two months ago.

Happiness expanded inside Kassidy that it had come to pass, that she was carrying their baby and she was going to give that precious gift to these two men she loved so much.

"What should we name her?" she asked.

Chris and Dag both laughed. "Her?" they said.

She grinned. "It could be a girl."

"You want a girl, babe?" Dag laid his palm on her stomach.

"I'm supposed to say I just want a healthy baby, but I kind of do want a little girl."

"A little girl would be awesome."

"But I really do just want a healthy baby," she added. "Boys can be fun too, and since he'll have two dads, I won't have to worry that I don't know how to entertain him."

"We'll take him to strip clubs," Dag said. "And teach him how to shoot tequila."

Kassidy giggled and gave him a little punch. "Right."

"Hey," he said. "Those are important things in a man's life. Along with hookers, fast cars and guns."

Kassidy stared at him in horror. "Hookers?" Her forehead tightened. "You've never gone to a hooker, have you?"

"Fuck no. I'm kidding, babe. About the guns too. Fast cars, maybe not."

"Oh. For a minute there I was having second thoughts about this."

Dag nuzzled her neck and Chris laughed. "You know he's full of shit."

"November." Dag sighed. "That's not far."

"About nine months," Kassidy said, trying not to smile, and earned herself a tickle.

"Can we have sex?" Chris asked.

"Right this minute?"

His lips twitched. "I meant for the next nine months."

"Christ," Dag said. "Please say yes."

"God yes," Kassidy said. "But even if we couldn't, you two still could with each other. Major benefit of a poly relationship. However, I've already Googled it and learned all about sex while pregnant. Apparently there's increased blood flow to your pelvic area during pregnancy, which can make your genitals swell and heighten sexual sensation."

Dag blanched. "My genitals are gonna swell?"

Kassidy giggled. "I certainly hope so. But no more than usual. Come on, follow along here. *My* genitals may swell."

"Christ," Chris said.

"However, some women report they can't orgasm as easily."

"We'll just have to try harder," Dag vowed.

"Thank you," she said demurely. "I appreciate that. Apparently, many couples find they feel more pleasure from foreplay, oral sex or masturbation than intercourse. So lots of foreplay would be good."

The two guys gave each other evil grins.

"Assuming I don't have morning sickness," she continued. "Because barfing during sex is not, well, sexy."

"Uh...no."

"But it's supposedly important to keep some level of intimacy going throughout pregnancy, to keep the relationship healthy but also to prevent sexual problems after the baby is born."

Chris frowned. "Why would we have sexual problems after the baby is born?"

"Possibly because after I give birth I will not want you to touch me ever again."

Both guys' jaws dropped.

"Kidding! Sort of. Seriously, it might take a while after the baby's born before I'm ready to have sex again—with one man, never mind two! You two could get antsy. But then again, you have each other, which takes some pressure off me." She beamed at them. "This is going to work out great. Not only that—three of us to take turns with diapers and middle of the night feedings."

Other Books by Kelly Jamieson

Heller Brothers Hockey

Breakaway

Faceoff

One Man Advantage

Hat Trick

Offside

Power Series

Power Struggle

Taming Tara

Power Shift

Rule of Three Series

Rule of Three

Rhythm of Three

Reward of Three

San Amaro Singles

With Strings Attached

How to Love

Slammed

Windy City Kink

Sweet Obsession

All Messed Up

Playing Dirty

Brew Crew

Limited Time Offer

No Obligation Required

Aces Hockey

Major Misconduct

Off Limits

Icing

Top Shelf

Back Check

Slap Shot

Playing Hurt

Big Stick

Game On

Last Shot

Body Shot

Hot Shot

Long Shot

Bayard Hockey

Shut Out

Cross Check

Wynn Hockey

Play to Win

In It To Win It

Win Big

For the Win

Stand Alone

Three of Hearts

Loving Maddie from A to Z

Dancing in the Rain

Love Me

Love Me More

Friends with Benefits

2 Hot 2 Handle

Lost and Found

One Wicked Night

Sweet Deal

Hot Ride

Crazy Ever After

All I Want for Christmas

Sexpresso Night

Irish Sex Fairy

Conference Call

Rigger

You Really Got Me

How Sweet It Is

Screwed

Firecracker

About the Author

Kelly Jamieson is a best-selling author of over forty romance novels and novellas. Her writing has been described as "emotionally complex", "sweet and satisfying" and "blisteringly sexy." She likes coffee (black), wine (mostly white), shoes (high heels) and hockey!

Subscribe to her newsletter for updates about her new books and what's coming up.

Find out what's new…
www.kellyjamieson.com
info@kellyjamieson.com